W9-DGL-476

Louise Farmer Smith

ONE HUNDRED YEARS OF MARRIAGE

A NOVEL IN STORIES

This is a work of fiction. References to real people, events, or locales are intended only to provide a sense of authenticity, and are used fictitiously. All other characters, and all incidents and dialogue, are drawn from the author's imagination and are not to be construed as real.

ISBN-10: 1468173758
ISBN-13: 9781468173758

For my gracious, loving mother,
Virginia Storm Farmer, in her 98th year.

PUBLISHED EXCERPTS

"The House After it Was Leveled" was published online in 2006 by *The Writing Site* under the title, "One Hundred Years of Marriage." www.writingsite.com/

"Return to Lincoln" was published Spring 2004 by *Bellevue Literary Review* which honored it with a Pushcart Nomination. blr.med.nyu.edu/

ACKNOWLEDGEMENTS

I am in debt to my New York and Washington writing groups who have read my work and kept up my courage while I grew into a writer: Eva Mekler, Nancy Kline, Susan Sindell, Betsy Mangan, Susan Malus, Mina Samuels, Anne Korkeakivi, Ronna Wineberg, Fiona Mackintosh, Wendy Mitman Clarke, Jan Linley, Melanie McDonald, and Gimbiya Kettering.

I want also to thank my wise and generous teachers, Maureen Brady, Martha Hughes, Gail Godwin, Richard Bausch, and Susan Richards Shreve.

For decades of patient and generous tech support, I thank my son, Timothy K. Smith.

My friend Ann Starr, writer, artist and critic, has countless times buoyed my sinking spirits with her trust in my imagination.

For precious space and time I must thank Virginia Center for the Creative Arts and Ragdale Foundation, serene refuges for artists.

And my gratitude is overflowing to my husband, Larry K Smith, who cooked a thousand suppers so that I could go on writing.

FAMILY TREE

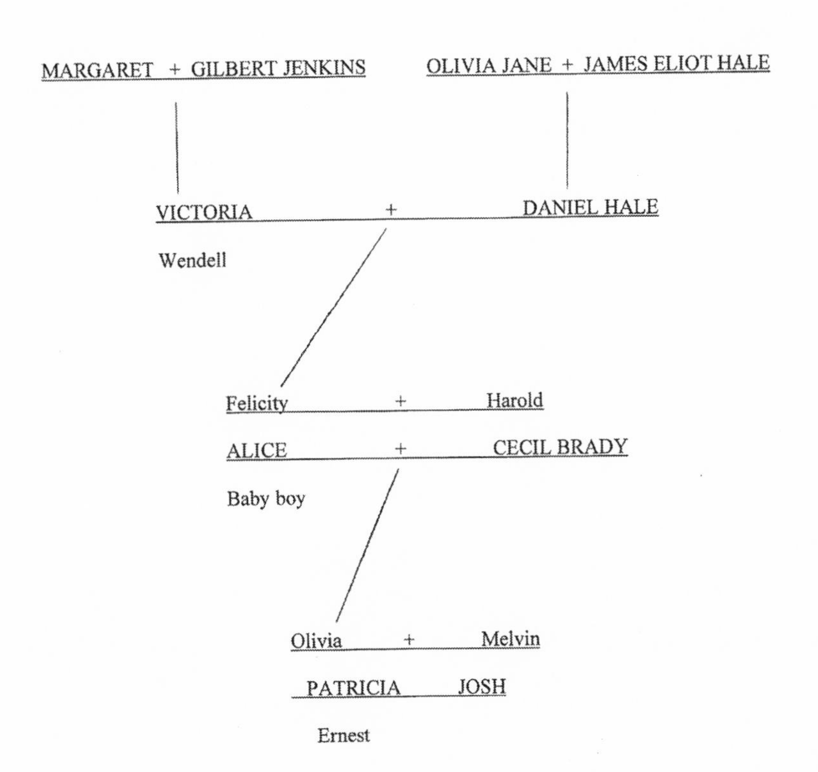
MARGARET + GILBERT JENKINS
OLIVIA JANE + JAMES ELIOT HALE
VICTORIA + DANIEL HALE
Wendell
Felicity + Harold
ALICE + CECIL BRADY
Baby boy
Olivia + Melvin
PATRICIA JOSH
Ernest

ORDER OF STORIES

Note to the reader:

What was your father thinking the night he proposed to your mother? Why did she say yes? By the time we ask, all the compelling details have cooled into whatever myths they've chosen to tell us. Our grandparents' stories are even more frozen, and the truths of our great-grandparents' unions have perished in the airless memories of the dead.

ONE HUNDRED YEARS OF MARRIAGE

THE HOUSE AFTER IT WAS LEVELED
1960

It looked like the four of us might eat supper without talking about Mother's situation, but before he picked up his fork, Daddy laid both palms on the table, and cleared his throat in his commanding way, bringing the meeting to order. Although he was a small man, someone had once told him he looked like General Patton and, at times like this I could see him swelling into the belief that he did. He'd left the army as a major, but Olivia and I called him The General.

"We're going to have to stay very organized during the next—well, as long as it takes," he announced.

"What's she got?" Ernest asked, looking up from his hash. He was twelve, a very tall boy with catsup in the corner of his mouth and the big eyes of a child who expects the grown-ups to clear everything up for him.

"Shh, she's sleeping now," The General said.

I was nineteen, the oldest, and Ernest looked at me thinking I would be the one to tell our daddy that Mama had sobbed off and on all day, gasping as though she were in pain. But I kept quiet.

"So we must each volunteer for broader assignments," The General said.

"I'll do the laundry," sixteen-year-old Olivia said, grabbing a job she could take care of and take off.

"Fine," I said. "I'll look after Mother and do the cooking."

"The trash," Ernest said. "And the mowing. I could mow, right, Daddy?"

"Okay," my father said. "But you've got to be a lot more careful with the edger than you have been. What you want is to get a slanted edge to the grass along the sidewalks. Like the bevel on a watch crystal. The edging is as important as the mowing."

"I can be careful. What's wrong with Mama?"

"Ernest," The General snapped. "This is not the kind of thing—This is not the measles!"

Ernest's pointy shoulders jerked up toward his ears. "I just asked."

"It's the Change, Ernest," Olivia said.

Ernest's eyes and mouth opened wide. "She won't change into anything, will she?" he asked. "She won't get mean?"

"Ernest, that's enough," The General said, growing red in the face. "Your mother is simply going through a time when—" He did a little throat clearing, "—when a woman's family has to make allowances until she's her old self again." The General gave Olivia a glare for her contribution to this outbreak.

We lived in a very old house my grandfather, Dan Hale and his father George Eliot, had built on his family's original claim—living room, dining room, music room and two bedrooms on the first floor, another bedroom up the stairs on the right and an unfinished storage space through a little door on the left. The town and the University had grown toward us through the years, and we were now surrounded by a very ordinary neighborhood. All that was left of the farm was a neglected orchard in back.

I was going to be a sophomore at the University next fall, and had the whole summer to get my formerly cheerful and frankly alluring mother back on her feet. It seemed right that I, the oldest, should do it, as I was the only member of the family who could stand to watch her cry. I myself never cried, and, I confess, that summer I couldn't understand why she didn't just take a walk around the block to clear her head. Daddy, who had been an army ordnance officer in charge of keeping all the Jeeps, trucks and tanks running, certainly expected people to shape up, buckle down, and carry on. We kids had been raised that way, each one pulling his own weight. On the other hand, I knew Mother was truly embarrassed to be lying in bed when she wasn't really sick.

Days passed and then weeks as the heat of that Oklahoma summer moved in and stayed. The family tightened ranks, treating each other with greater courtesy, being more careful not to leave a dirty sock on the bathroom floor or a milky glass in the kitchen sink. Every Saturday Ernest mowed and trimmed and mowed again, coming into the kitchen red-faced and shining with sweat, wanting The General to come inspect his slanted edges. My father loved work—pursued it, sucked it toward himself, or manufactured it when it wasn't readily available. Family legend held that my father could fix a car with wire off a fence post and wasn't above scavenging at the dump for machinery to repair during his college years. For my parents, Depression survivors, work was the only way out of trouble. But in spite of everything we did, Mother got worse, curling her body away, even from me.

∾∾

The last Saturday in June, as soon as I'd vacuumed and made the Jello, I stuck my head in the front bedroom. "I'm gonna run a quick errand," I said. Mother, her eyes widening, sat up in bed and gripped the edge of the sheet. Finally she managed a little smile. "Sure, darlin', take your time." I rushed to the library and came back with an armload of books. Obviously work was not the answer. Maybe I could read my way out of trouble.

The next morning Mama insisted we all leave her and go to church. We sat in our usual three-quarters-of-the-way-down-on-the-left pew, and I realized except for the library I hadn't been out of the house during the day for three weeks. After the benediction, as the organ swelled and the congregation peeled their sweating bottoms off the pews and began to chat, I stood to look around for my boyfriend, Tom, to remind myself what he looked like in the daylight.

I tried to glance about inconspicuously. My bosom rose and fell as I scanned the milling congregation for Tom. I was a little self-conscious about having a bust measurement for a girl four inches taller. I stood just as Mother had taught me—waist drawn back taking all the bow out of my spine. Thank heavens the stick-out slips and waist-makers had gone out in high school. Now, in my chemise, standing carefully, bottom tucked under, bosom pulled back, I could still pass for a straight, modest Methodist.

Shoot! Instead of Tom, I saw Mrs. Eugenia Pryor coming against the crowd down the center aisle, waving to catch my eye. I pretended not to see her and turned to shepherd my bunch back toward the other end of our pew, but The General, seeing the center aisle to be the most efficient route to the exit, made a two-handed sawing gesture like an M.P. diverting a convoy, and we three kids turned back around to face the oncoming Pryor.

"Patricia, dear, we've missed your sweet mother," she said resting her hands on the backs of the pews effectively plugging up our escape route. "The Women's Society of Christian Service. The Sunday School Committee. We hardly know how to turn the lights on around here without her. How many Sundays has it been?"

"Mrs. Pryor," I exclaimed, "where'd you get that lovely hat?"

"Is she sick?" Mrs. Pryor asked.

"Oh, she's all right. This heat is getting to all of us."

"So she's all right then?" This question she addressed to Ernest behind me.

I turned to watch his little Adam's apple bob.

As the official church visitor, the one in charge of knowing what every Methodist was doing on Sunday morning, Mrs. Pryor was also a one-woman cheerleading team for Reverend Mapple, and I knew the only thing that distracted her from other people's business was an opportunity to promote her man. "I really wish Mother *had* been here," I rushed to say. "That sermon! Boy, was he wound up."

"An absolute human dynamo!" Mrs. Pryor avowed, her eyes rising to the stained glass windows.

"We are blessed," I said, turning to push Ernest out the now empty aisle. The General and Olivia had already fled.

∾ ∾

That summer Ernest had trouble getting organized. Although he seemed shy about talking to Mother, he also seemed anxious about being away from her for very long. He didn't fish for crawdads in the University golf course pond or visit the Biology Building to gape at the formaldehyde bottles of two-headed calf fetuses and diseased brains. Olivia, however, didn't have any trouble being out of the house. Morning after morning I'd come into the kitchen to make breakfast and see her folding up the ironing board, giving me a big smile as she grabbed the hangers of shirts and blouses to deliver to our closets before she sailed out the door with her tennis racket.

I heard Ernest quietly phoning his friend R. B., inviting him over to help build an orange crate canoe, a project Ernest had started in our storage room last winter after finding a tiny blueprint in *Boy's Life.* Ernest put the phone down quietly. "R.B. says oranges don't come in crates anymore."

"It's kind of a hot project for summer," I said. "And when you leave the storage room door open, I just about choke on the dust."

"I can't help that. If I close it, I can't breathe."

∾ ∾

Meals were no problem. There was nothing much to do but check the cans of salmon, tuna, and corned beef hash, the catsup, cereal, and milk. If anyone missed Mother's cooking, they were too polite to mention it. I carried her meals to their room and arranged the old embroidered footstool so she could sit up straight on the edge of the bed to eat. I sat on the dresser bench to keep her company.

As she struggled to swallow the lunch, we both listened to the bam of Ernest's hammer in the storage room. Lately each blow was answered by a faint shower of plaster in the walls of the bedroom. There were dry pockets in the soft green wallpaper that were now filling up with crumbled bits. Bam, bam, the hammer sounded; shhh, the plaster fell. I glanced up at Mother. "I don't care," she said. "He can knock the whole house down as long as he's happy up there. Where's Olivia?"

"Tennis."

"Good."

Olivia was our golden girl, a blond beauty, tan, and athletic, whereas I was brunette, freckled and couldn't get enthusiastic about playing anything in the broiling Oklahoma sun.

"Mama," I said and pulled the dresser bench closer to the side of the bed, "didn't Aunt Fel go through the Change? She's your own sister. Wouldn't she know what you should take?"

"Oh, Fel had a few hot flashes. We laughed. Felicity could always handle everything better than I could." She put an arm behind to support herself, bowed her head and stared down at the bed. In the noontime heat she appeared to be melting.

"I could call her."

"No. It'd just cause a big, you know."

She was afraid Aunt Felicity would tell Grandma Vic whose angina would kick up if she knew her younger daughter was in trouble.

I took the plate. She'd eaten almost nothing.

◦◦

"What are all those books?" Ernest asked after everyone else had gone to bed. He had a glass of milk in his hand and stood in the living room in his faded pajama bottoms. From where I sat in my usual corner under the yellow light of the floor lamp, I could watch through the bay window, and had already seen a midnight blue motorcycle slide silently into place under the elm trees that protected our street.

"It's nearly twelve," I said.

"You look dressed up," he said looking at my Madras sundress.

"I'm thinking of turning in soon."

"So, what're you reading?" In the shadowy corner where he stood, his body was so thin, his chest so hairless, he looked like a turtle without its shell.

"This is Freud. I'm reading about hysteria."

"Hysteria like laughing?"

I looked at my watch. "It's long past your bedtime."

"It's summer."

"Good night, Ernest."

After the last sound from Ernest's bedroom I waited another twenty minutes before I walked out the back door, down the driveway and climbed on the back of the motorcycle. Tom walked the cycle to the end of the block, and we glided off into the night, not stopping until we coasted to the back door of his boarding house on the other side of town. Inside the house, he carried me up the creaking back stairs, so we'd sound like one person to the ears of his landlady, who slept in a downstairs bedroom.

Tom and I had first met in church. He had that rock-solid masculine confidence and good humor small town Oklahoma could turn out when it wanted to. He'd been away in the army since graduating from the University and was now back finishing up law school. He was nine years older than I was, but his big grin and corny humor made him seem like a kid.

He laid me out on the bed and slipped off my flats. "So, how're you doin'?" he whispered as he bent to set my shoes quietly on the floor. I smiled and shrugged, eager to get past the pleasantries he always insisted upon. "Your folks and everybody doin' fine?" He knew my folks and liked them, and they liked him, but he hadn't heard about Mother's collapse, which let me keep my family separate from all that happened in this room. This patchwork quilt I lay on was for me a shaded pool within the flat, dry plain of my everyday life.

"Fine, fine, fine, Tom. We're all just fine." I was wet and jittery and weary from longing for him all day. He stood by the bed, leisurely assessing my frame, fitting his hand over my hip bone as though figuring how best to get a good grip.

That spring I had given up my virginity to Tom without nearly as much moral turmoil as I had anticipated. Then, and each time afterward, he provided a Trojan prophylactic and brushed away my offense at his forethought. "A good Boy Scout is always prepared, Patricia."

Tonight the muscle in my stomach tightened, arcing me up to kiss him, but he wouldn't be hurried. "Patticake, don't rush us. This is part of it." Laying one hand on my chest and another on my thigh to flatten me, he stood like a man at an ironing board, coolly assessing his work. I struggled against his pressing palms.

He frowned. "Is that nonskid lipstick?" Just like him to joke when I was getting desperate. Like a turtle on her back, I craned my neck. He liked to kiss, and I knew it. Light as a cat he could snuggle, must have been born knowing how, a gift from God like his dimples and his tidy body—just the right height for me—but this cool eye he was putting on made me want to scream. But just then I heard footsteps and jerked my head back to check the door hook he'd installed at my request. He cupped a hand gently over my mouth. Every thump and creak in that old house signaled the arrival of the police and Mrs. Pryor leading the Methodists, come to drag me away for my sinfulness.

The footsteps passed our door and went on down the hall. Mohammed, one of the hundreds of North African engineering students on campus, kept Mediterranean hours. I was safe, but the boundaries of my security here were wrecked. I rolled toward the wall, my hands over my hot face.

Tom did not protest or cajole. He was up, looking for something in his closet. He came back with an army blanket which he rolled and, with some fussiness, arranged as a pillow against the iron foot board, then, shifting me as though I were nothing more than a sack of feed, he lay himself down on the outer edge of the narrow bed facing me from the other end. I wrapped my arm around his sock feet to help anchor us to the little bed.

"Did you hear the one about the guy and girl sittin' on the fence watchin' the bull and the cow?" he whispered.

"What is it," I hissed, "with you and the barnyard?"

He shrugged and lay his head to the side in a boyish way that always turned me on. "Gee, Patricia, I'm just not up to the classy taste of a county seat girl like yourself."

"Come on. You're going to be a lawyer in another semester."

"You think lawyers have high minds?"

"Well, you can't tell a joke like that at the country club."

"That's where I heard it. Professor Rutherford told it. Now the guy and girl are sittin' on the fence watchin' the ruttin', and the guy says, 'Boy, I wish I was doin' that.' And the girl says, 'Go ahead. It's your cow.'"

I clamped my hand over my mouth to hide a smile. "Oh, Lordy, Tom, are you just being naughty so I'll scold you? Don't make me be your mother."

"Never, Patticake, never." He rose up on his knees and took my ankles in either hand to drag me down the bed, pulling my head off the pillow, and spreading my legs. "Not what I had in mind," he said.

∾ ∾

Throughout the heat of July, Olivia, Ernest and I maintained scrupulous attention to our duties. When I wasn't sitting by Mother's bed or cooking, I read up on depression, menopause, existentialism, and psychoanalysis. I consulted the great thinkers I'd heard about as a freshman: Sigmund Freud, Dietrich Bonhoeffer, Paul Tillich, as well as *Ladies' Home Journal*.

Daddy, of course, went to work every day as City Engineer, served on the church finance board, and discharged his duties as Republican town chairman. At home he repaired the gutters, cleaned out kitchen drawers, and rearranged all the coils of wire and cable into a new pattern on the garage wall. It was hard for someone who'd commanded a whole battalion of men in Korea to settle for being in charge of so few people. He inspected our work, commended us for our performance, shined his shoes, brushed his suits and went to meetings. Sometimes I would see him standing before his highboy mirror carefully arranging his heavy graying curls. The last time I saw him so deeply involved in this activity while Mother lay right there in the double bed they shared, her eyes staring at the ceiling, desperate for relief, I had imagined myself clocking him with a monkey wrench.

∾ ∾

For all my reading I still could not figure out how to help Mother. When I'd come in, her face would be a great puddle, eyes full, cheeks soaked and often panting from a wave of heat generated from inside her. She seemed to be trying hard not to move at all. God, for her was the Great Physician, and she believed if she lay still enough, prayed without demand, hoped without vision, opened her heart to Him, He would take mercy and raise her up. She read from a book entitled, *Let Go and Let God.* When she was sleeping, I slipped it from her fingers.

> The only complete and sure cure for your bad nerves, as you call them, is to relax in the hands of God and know that He is now looking after your troubles, that He is now guiding you into the quiet waters of inner peace.

The book shook in my hand. All my life I'd choked down such language and imposed it on others as I led devotionals at church. But now, standing beside her bed, seeing between her eyebrows the crease that didn't smooth out even in sleep, I realized my mother's strengths—determination, initiative, creativity—were being paralyzed by what amounted to religious knockout drops. Surely God didn't want her mindless, helpless, in total surrender, not even taking responsibility for her own troubles. Surely ours was the God who helped those who helped themselves. I hid the book in the back of my closet.

When she stirred, I was standing there. I watched her hand search the bed beside her. "Have you seen my book?"

I spoke softly, trying to sound casual. "You know, Mama, the ideas in that book sound good, but maybe they're for a person with another kind of problem, someone who's too high on himself, arrogant, whose ego is getting between him and God's will. Your poor little ego couldn't get between you and a breeze."

"No, no. I've been too proud," she blurted, "trying to handle everything myself. For years I've been praying God would change Daddy, make him calm, a more loving person." Her face broke, red and rubbery. "I'm the one who needs to change. I need to learn to wait on the Lord. God promised. Marcus Mapple says we underestimate God."

"But maybe Rev. Mapple meant that another way."

"Oh, please, darlin', let me have the book. Please."

All I'd ever wanted to be was the one who made her happy. Obediently, I went for the book and gave it to her. Her breathing calmed; she patted my hand to let me know it was all right to leave her alone. I felt dizzy as though spinning in a swing.

As I quietly slipped out of her room, Ernest burst in the front door, panting. "Patty, I need a ride! Fast! They're unpacking a huge refrigerator in the alley behind the biology building."

I grabbed my purse and keys. We piled into the Buick and sped off to the campus. Finding the thin slats needed for the canoe walls was getting harder and harder for Ernest, who searched alone through alleys and trash heaps. We got to the alley where he'd seen the refrigerator being unpacked, but the crate was gone. At the far end of the alley, we saw a huge trash truck turning the corner, noisily changing gears, accelerating, bearing away the precious building materials.

"Step on it!" Ernest yelled.

We were a mile out of town on a two-lane highway before I could pull alongside the speeding truck. Ernest hung out the passenger window, pushing his gangly body up high enough to be seen by the driver. "Stop! Stop! Please!"

The driver helped us rip the crate apart to get it into the Buick's big trunk.

At home with a bundle of slats under each arm, I climbed up into the thick heat of the storage room. There, between the banks of taped-up boxes, cast-off toys and abandoned art projects, propped on sawhorses and old chairs, running fifteen feet long, was the skeleton of the Orange Crate Canoe. I was aghast.

"Big isn't it?" Ernest said, beaming.

"Ernest, it's huge. Did you know?"

He shrugged. "The plans made it look little. I thought, something just big enough for me. But look. We can all get in."

I was looking at it, all right, and it was plain the swell of its widest part could never pass through the little door to the storage room. "Ernest, honey, it's so hot up here. You must roast."

"Yeah," he made a tiny smile, embarrassed by his situation. "I take off everything but my underpants."

"You don't have to do this, work in all this heat. You could wait for fall or just chuck the whole project."

"I wanted to, but Daddy said he'd be very disappointed if I didn't finish what I started."

"Have you shown it to him?"

"I'm waiting until I get some of the walls on."

~

As I pushed through Freud's *An Outline of Psycho-Analysis,* reading and rereading the clinical language, looking up in the dictionary at least four words on every page, I'd grown more and more sure that this Viennese doctor wouldn't give two hoots about the pressures on an Oklahoma woman. But when I came upon the line, "Holding back aggressiveness is in general unhealthy and leads to illness," I hugged that little library book to my chest. Mama was the perfect example. To her way of thinking, the role of women was to be a great sponge of aggression, just soaking up the poison men spewed out, thereby keeping the environment clean and safe for children. The problem was Mama was now over-saturated.

She'd always behaved as though The General's temper, always so close to the surface, was her responsibility. She'd dance around, cooing and patting his sleeve—"Now Cecil, don't concern yourself." "I'm sorry for this, Cecil," she'd apologize for the traffic or a story in the newspaper or someone else's ill-judged comment, trying sweetly, frantically to keep the lid on, never getting angry herself. Aggressiveness in women was, after all, in poor taste. Every time I watched this, I wanted to scream.

"Mama, what are you angry about?" I asked when she'd had some morning coffee.

"Nothing," she gasped, stricken I'd suggest such a thing. The room was already hot, and the smell of plaster dust burned my nose.

"You're sure? Something long ago, maybe?"

"Oh, darlin', I had the most marvelous childhood." She relaxed back on the pillow smiling. "So many sweet people loved me, and my parents had a wonderful marriage. Never once raised their voices in anger."

"Didn't Grandma Vic ever complain that Granddad wouldn't get a job?"

"Never. Not once. She always took up for him."

I'd heard all this before and knew what was coming, but I listened more carefully this time.

"Once, during the Depression," she began, "times were so desperate. I've told you. We had three grown cousins down on their luck living with us. I was in college, working full time, trying to help feed everyone, and I heard about a teaching job Daddy would have been perfect for, but he wouldn't even go see about it. I yelled at him. 'How can you just sit there, when there's no food in this house!' Mother heard me, and she got up out of her sick bed to come in and say to me, 'Alice, I'm ashamed of you, talking that way to your sweet father.'"

I never liked that little snippet of family history, always told to laud my grandparents' perfect marriage. "Don't you get tired of staying quiet when Daddy starts yelling?"

A chill passed over her face, and I knew I'd gone too far. I stared at her through the thick air, and she looked back as unsmiling as I was. Finally I asked, "Have you had any dreams lately you can remember?"

∾ ∾

By the end of July I realized I no longer had any friends. The girlfriends from high school who'd called for a movie or a swim at the beginning of the summer didn't even call to talk. I wouldn't, of course, have talked to them about Mama. Everyone knew you weren't supposed to talk about family matters outside the home. Of course, at our house, we didn't talk about family matters inside the home either, and the only secrets that were mine to tell were about sins I had committed myself or misfortunes that had befallen me. It was best, of course, not to talk about these either.

Poor Ernest banged away every day in an airless room, as though he was actually going to have something to carry him down a river one day. And my own project—Mother's recovery—seemed just as doomed. I felt her sinking as though into a subterranean vault, lying still, waiting for the sod to cover her.

She spoke sometimes of her beloved grandmother, Olivia Jane Hale, a woman who pioneered first in Nebraska, then in Oklahoma, living in a dugout. Ever since I'd been a little girl, this woman had been my model, a distant star of perfection. "The sweetest creature who ever lived," Mother said, "What an angel, never raised her voice or argued or spoke ill of anyone, and if someone was criticized in her presence, she would come to his rescue: "Wendell may be a little shiftless, as you say, but he's so pleasant to be around."

The greatest compliment I was ever given was years ago when my Aunt Fel said of me to Mama, "She's going to be another Olivia Jane."

Oh no! I thought now. Not another sweet, long-suffering woman. Surely there was another great grandmother back there in time I could take after. I knew nothing about Grandma Vic's mother except that her name was Margaret and she was from North Carolina. Maybe she was a real southern belle, fiery like Scarlett O'Hara.

∾ ∾

I lay on Tom with my total, sex-drugged weight, our bare bodies sealed with sweat. There was no breeze through the open window, and we breathed a thick mixture of each other's odors. "Tom?" I looked up into his eyes. "I need to ask you a question."

"Shoot," he said. I could hear his heart's deep, steady ka-thumping and wished I were a girl with nothing on her mind.

"How do you feel about anger?" I asked. "I mean people getting really mad, yelling at each other, saying mean, exaggerated, hurtful things."

With both hands he lifted my heavy face from his chest. "Patty, are you angry at me?"

"No, never!"

"Cause if you are, let's get on the cycle right now and head for the woods, so we can wrestle and yell."

"Oh, Tom." I could see it: Tom and me crashing around in the trees, him tearing my clothes and me throwing him off and standing my ground, spitting it all out, every big hurt and petty aggravation about my family, hurled into his teeth—everything, including that excruciatingly long list of those things that weren't mine to tell.

I laid my head back down and panted, my cheek slipping minutely back and forth in the sweat that sealed me to his chest hair. I wanted to marry him right then, and my throat tightened as it might have if I were going to cry.

Mother's crying had dried to a silent, black grief that felt contagious. The other members of the family began avoiding each other. Olivia finished her laundry duties earlier and earlier. Ernest stayed in the storage room, sometimes working. I could hardly get out of bed in the mornings. The General did not mention my malingering.

~

"You're going to the doctor, Mother!" Freud had completely let me down. His explanation for weak egos in women—feeling inadequate regarding their plumbing. Ridiculous!

"Oh, darlin', I'd be too ashamed to face Dr. Tilghman."

"So I'll call another doctor."

"No, no, I just need to be patient and stop telling God what he should—"

"Mother, maybe God wants *me* to decide what we should do."

She looked shocked but didn't answer back.

Dr. Whittle, usually our third choice, put her in the hospital and prescribed sedatives. "We've got to help her shut off all this crying," he said.

The General visited her every evening alone. Afterwards, he said he drove around for a long time to clear his head. So I imagined they discussed important matters, things about their marriage. I didn't ask, of course. When I visited her in the afternoons, she was asleep or too groggy to make much sense.

The hospital was on Tom's side of town, and I always managed to drive past his boarding house, going and coming. I knew I wouldn't see him, but it was a comfort to see the motorcycle leaning against the garage and think of him at his desk in the back, his sleeves rolled up tight, perhaps stopping now and then to think of me. In the daylight the street looked pretty poor. A few other boarding houses and some bungalows slumped behind unkempt, junky yards.

One afternoon as I cruised down this street, I saw my father and Olivia on a porch. I pressed the horn before I saw that it wasn't Olivia, just a young woman who had the same long blond hair. He was holding her hand in both of his. I floor-boarded the Buick.

Unbelievable! Another woman. Driving around to clear his head, huh? This secret side of him and whatever it meant was what Mama must lay buried under. An outsider might have said I had very little evidence, but that scene at that shabby house shifted so much of what I had taken for granted, I knew there was a lot more to discover.

Should I tell Olivia what I'd seen on Kemper Street? Shoot, Olivia was probably onto him years ago and knew tons of stuff I didn't. Keeping it from me could be what kept her step so light.

~

Under the kitchen window in back of our house was a hiding place. As a little girl I figured out that if I sat on the box that housed the gas meter, no one could see me when they looked casually from the driveway because of the way the enclosed back porch stuck out. And if someone glanced out the window, they'd look right over my head. I had remembered this as a high perch from which my legs dangled down, so I was surprised how low it was now.

I listened to my father's car pull in beside the Buick, and I heard him inhale as he opened the screened door to the back porch. His keys dropped, clank, on the dryer as usual. Then nothing. He was searching the rooms, not calling my name, just quietly looking for me. I waited.

It was getting towards supper time, and I could hear him begin to open some cans and bang pans, but I didn't rush in to help, just leaned back on the white clapboards and gazed into the long shadows gathering in the old orchard. The happiest time of my life was the Second World War when my father was away in the Philippines. I was four years old when Mama returned to the house she'd grown up in. Her sister, Aunt Felicity, had moved in as well with her two kids and their little dog, Fluffy because Uncle Harold had shipped out to Italy. We used to play war right there in the orchard. Harold Jr., seven years older than me, taught us to goose step and salute like Nazis and to make the screaming-bloody-murder cry of a kamikaze pilot crashing into one of our carriers. Fluffy went wild when Howard, up in a gnarled old peach tree, bombed us girls with green peaches.

Aunt Fel and my mother taught us kids to do the Charleston and play ukuleles. They peeled all the old greasy paper off the walls in the kitchen and put up big, beautiful pink roses. The man at the store had told them that rose wallpaper was meant for bedrooms, but they put it up anyway and painted the woodwork pink. Then they took Grandmother Brady's old walnut china cabinet and painted it pink too and the round oak table—pink like a birthday cake sittin' there in the middle of our rosy kitchen. They said they were wild women. They laughed like crazy and had to put down their paintbrushes to wipe their tears and blow their noses.

Scraping sounds of spoons getting the last of the stew out of the bowls let me know it was time to leave the meter box and go inside. I'd heard The General tell Olivia and Ernest I was at my friend Deanna's. I hoped he thought I had hanged myself.

I slipped in the back door and smiled at Olivia and Ernest. My father's eyes were wide and he was breathing through his mouth. I went to the sink and began to scrub the pan.

"Let me do that, Patricia," he said. "Then we can take a walk." I hung onto the pan when he tried to pull it away. He raced around the kitchen, snatching the bowls from in front of Olivia and Ernest. I worked slowly at the sink, all but sterilizing each dish before I put it in the dishwasher.

"Want a Dairy Queen?" Olivia whispered to Ernest and within thirty seconds the Buick roared out the driveway. My father and I were alone in the kitchen.

"Let's sit at the table, Patricia," a thin version of his commanding officer voice said, trying to make me a child about to be disciplined. He'd spanked me after I was twelve—old enough to be totally humiliated. "You need to understand some things," he said. "The city is widening Kemper Street. As city engineer I have had to visit every property owner. I can show you the blueprints at the office. Please sit down."

Still facing the sink, I slowly dried my hands on a tea towel. "No," I said.

"Why not? I need to talk to you." He spoke to my left and when I turned my head away, he danced to my right. "Kemper is going to become part of Route Nine." He wasn't angry. Panic was what I was hearing, and I gripped the cold edge of the sink, fighting the urge to relent and sooth his panic as he expected any of us to do.

"The city owns the land the trees are on, but, as a courtesy—You saw me saying goodbye to one of the property owners. Please sit down."

He didn't know how much I knew, that it was only a glance: His shoulder had been against the screened door. His hat was off, maybe still in the car the city provided to him during business hours. He'd held her hands in both of his, his head cocked to the side, a lingering gesture, tenderness I'd never seen.

"No." I still did not turn around.

"We can't just not talk," he growled.

I whirled around. "Sure we can not talk! Nobody in this family talks."

His jaw hinge was working, throbbing like a heart. I'd never yelled at him before. "What do you want me to do?" he begged, palms up.

Do? What did he mean? I steadied myself on the back of a chair. He was offering something. Was there anything in the world that would help us? I took a deep breath, then gritted my teeth. "You could be a real daddy to Ernest. He looks up to you, slaves to get your attention and approval. And you do nothing but stay busy, busy, busy. He's suffering. He doesn't understand what's going on with this family. Pay him some attention, for Heaven's sake!" I was shaking.

Daddy eyes were wide and his mouth gaped.

"You can start by figuring out how to get Ernest's canoe out of the storage room."

"What's wrong? Can't he get it out?"

"It's fifteen feet long and too wide to come out that little door. "

"Does Earnest know it's too big to come out?"

"I'm sure he does. He's just working away, embarrassed, hoping we don't know."

He ran his hand through his curls and patted them into place. "We can't rip open the floor and spoil the bedroom ceiling. He'll have to take it apart."

"No. The whole canoe, safely outside. You figure it out." I left the kitchen.

∾ ∾

News had gotten around town that Alice Brady, church pillar and model citizen, was back home from the hospital, mysteriously confined to her bed. Mama's friend, Angela Worth, had been stopping by regularly with food or an offer to sit with Mama while I went out, but I didn't think she'd like the hours I wanted to be away, every night. I thanked her and promised to call if I needed anything. But other visitors knocked, fellow Methodists from our large congregation, a few I didn't even recognize. I caught some of them looking past my shoulder into the front room, eyeing my housekeeping.

The knocking on the door hammered Mother's body in a way Ernest's work never had. She lay still like a creature in hiding.

"Mother's sleeping. It'll mean a lot to her that you came by," I would tell them so they'd feel they got credit for this visit and wouldn't return. But the official church visitors, Mrs. Pryor and her sidekick, Mrs. Plottle, hung on like plaque, coming back every few days, so I finally let them in.

Mother's inability to eat much had stripped her of her curvaceous figure, leaving a skinny, adolescent body and a strangely youthful face dominated by her large wounded eyes. But her voice was as ravaged and full of scrapes and pockets of air as a ninety-year-old's. As I brushed out her auburn hair, the sight of her sharp little shoulder sticking out of the nightgown broke my heart. What kind of tribe subjected its weakest member to such painful rituals as church visitation? She managed to sit against her fluffed up pillows, and before I let the visitors into her room, I opened the blinds so the sunlight fell across the bed.

"How are we doing, dear?" Mrs. Pryor cooed. I resented these women, their careful footsteps, their funereal tones. I also suspected they were glad to see Alice Brady brought low and were looking for specific information they could carry away. I got them seated and turned up the big oscillating fan.

"Alice, honey, does this problem of yours have anything to do with the Change of Life?" Mrs. Pryor asked.

Mother smiled sadly. "Well, my life has certainly changed."

Mrs. Pryor looked over her glasses. "Don't you know what I mean, dear?" She glanced back at me as though Mother's little joke was a sign of ignorance or derangement.

"You know, Alice," Mrs. Pryor continued, "Doris Pettibone had a terrible time with the Change and had to have her uterus out. She required nine pints of blood, poor thing. They had to make a hundred calls to find O negative."

I watched the netting jiggle on Mrs. Pryor's hat as she spoke and watched her mouth work, puckered lips extended to enunciate her views. "Just think what a worry that would be your entire life to know you had rare blood. I hope your blood isn't rare, Alice. It isn't, is it?"

Mother was looking to me, and I knew I should never have let these women in.

Mrs. Pryor patted the bed to get Mama's attention, and gushed on. "It isn't rare, is it, your blood, Alice dear?"

"My blood?" Mama blurted and stared between Mrs. Pryor and Mrs. Plottle as though at a third guest. "It's common as grass, but poison! I've poisoned my whole family."

The front door opened and closed. Oh, God, let this be some rescue!

Olivia appeared in the bedroom doorway and, seeing who I had let in, frowned at me. "Well, hello everyone," she said brightly. Mama tried to sit up for Olivia who was in white shorts and held her tennis racket casually at her side. Across her rosy forehead sweat sealed some strands of her blond hair. She glowed in the sick room. I sensed a slight tremor between the visitors. Both women turned to stare at Olivia.

Mrs. Pryor straightened her shoulders and cleared her throat. "Olivia? Tennis?"

"Yes. I've been out playing tennis," my sister said, not giving an inch. Mrs. Pryor eyed Olivia's slim, tanned legs. Olivia strode across the room and shook hands. She loved their disapproval and, parking her tennis racket against her hip began to talk about this morning's game. Hooray, Olivia, I thought, we are not all dead.

I watched Mrs. Pryor give a nod to Mrs. Plottle to collect her vote, then she said, "Don't you think you're needed here at home, Olivia?"

"Oh no," Mother cried. "We need her to play tennis. It helps."

Mrs. Pryor returned her attention to Mama. "Now dear, I never heard of poison blood." She reached for Mama's hand.

"It's clotted," Mama wailed, pulling her hand away. "But that's better than bleeding in public, isn't it?" She looked at me for the answer. I didn't speak, and she covered her face with the sheet.

"I know you're suffering, honey," Mrs. Pryor said, "just like your dear mother all those years, continuing to paint china."

"My father was a n'er do well!" Mama croaked from under the sheet. I'd never heard her use that term in regard to Grandpa Dan, and I opened my mouth to say something to cover the silence, but Mrs. Pryor spoke first.

"Now, you know your dear father took care of her all those years."

"Yes," Mama's voice through the sheet was muffled, "never spoke a word of anger, either of them."

"And you have a wonderful, steady husband, too," Mrs. Pryor cooed.

Just then Ernest must have moved the canoe because there was a creaking from above. Mama peeked out from the sheet, and we all looked toward the ceiling. The visitors exchanged looks. *Perhaps this girl has another relative in the attic.*

"It's time for Mama to take her..."

"What *is* she taking?" Mrs. Pryor turned to ask.

Mama sat up and sobbed, "Lithium! Tell everyone."

"Oh, no," Mrs. Plottle cried, seizing her opportunity to make a contribution. "Isn't that the one that makes a woman grow a beard?"

Mama moaned and bowed her head. I pictured myself taking Mrs. Plottle by the throat, but at that moment, Ernest dropped something sharp between the rafters that pierced the ceiling plaster. A fine shower of white dust poured through the sunlight and onto Mother's head. The effect was ethereal. She sat up blinking and gasping as though called to attention by God. The church visitors were silent although Mrs. Pryor's mouth kept working as she gaped.

"We'd like to be alone now, ladies," I intoned, and the visitors flapped about for a moment, gathering their purses and adjusting their hats, then rushed away.

Mama came to supper in the dining room that night. Right after the blessing The General made his pre-speech clearing of the throat and announced, "The ventilation in this house is very poor. I believe all our problems can be solved with an attic fan. We'll have to cut a huge hole under the eave at the back of the house in order to install it. And, by the way, Ernest," he looked his only son in the eye, "that would be a golden opportunity for you and me to slide the canoe down into the back yard."

There was silence at the table. Ernest blinked like a boy walking out of prison. I patted the table next to my father's plate. "Good idea, Daddy."

The General stared at me, his eye brows up so high they'd disappeared under his silver curls. He was asking were we square now? Would this attic fan scheme secure my silence about what I'd seen across town? Oh, Daddy, I thought, you've only begun to secure my silence. "Can I have a ride in the canoe?" I asked Ernest. He grinned and his happiness flooded the room

He was still speechless and to cover his awkwardness, Olivia began to report on the visit from Mrs. Pryor and Mrs. Plottle. "Those ladies took off like you-know-whats out of you-know-where," she said. "You should have been there, Daddy, to see Mama face down Mrs. Pryor who doesn't think the daughters of shut-ins should play tennis."

We all laughed, but The General's laugh was his nervous, let's-all-settle-down laugh. Then he pressed his hands flat on the table and tapped his fingertips to bring the disorder to an end.

"It was just my needle-nosed pliers," Ernest said and we laughed some more.

"Those old biddies thought it was a sign from God," Olivia said. Ernest laughed so hard, he choked and sneezed milk out his nose.

"Let's just— Let's all just—" The General sputtered. I ignored him and began to reprise the whole rare blood harangue. Hearing his children make fun of church ladies caused my father to stand up, though he still bent to press his palms on the table. My recital picked up in its intensity. I exaggerated the tackiness of their hats and the persimmon pucker of their judgmental lips, then I squinted over imaginary glasses— "Do you have rare blood, dear?" The laughter got louder.

"I never did like either of those women," Mother admitted, and shock at this unprecedented candor pushed us towards hysteria. The General opened his mouth to hush her, but I shot him a look, and he sat back down.

"My guess is, God doesn't like them either," I said, looking at my father who took up ringing his spoon on his glass to restore order.

I sat on the edge of the bed and held out my bare foot for Tom to slip on my shoe. The night air was stifling. "I've lost you, Pat. Haven't seen you for weeks," Tom whispered.

I pulled my foot back. "What do you mean?"

"Where ya been? I feel like I'm alone. Like you're just using me each night."

"That's a terrible thing to say."

Holding a shoe in either hand he straightened. "We're not friends anymore like we used to be, Patty. I don't want to go on like this."

Oh, God! "Tom, *please*." I knew what he was talking about. But, of course, I couldn't explain my fears about Mama or my suspicions about The General—one more thing I wasn't supposed to talk about to anyone outside the family. My life had backed up into an airless tank, and I felt my secrets go rancid in my chest.

"Tom, I know I've been real quiet, but it doesn't have anything to do with us."

"Well, who then? 'Cause we don't seem to have a word to say to each other. I feel like you're mad at me, but when I try to find out anything, I hear some drifted-off woman mumbling. I might as well be in bed with a cigar store Indian!"

"*Please, Tom,*" I whispered.

He lifted my chin, and in the moonlight he looked me dead in the eye. I felt weak. "I can't talk about this, Tom."

"It must be important." He folded his arms, a shoe poking up from each elbow.

"Of course, it's important!" I snapped.

"Too important to tell me?"

I shrugged, then took a deep breath. "I'm terrified my mother's losing her mind." I clamped my hand over my mouth. Too late. "She got better, but now she's going under again."

"That's terrible." He laid the shoes on the bed and sat down beside me. "What makes you think this?"

"She cries all the time and can't get out of bed."

"Have you taken her to the doctor?"

"The doctor!" I shot back at him. "The doctor made her worse! We're all drowning." I gritted my teeth and tried to keep my voice low. "Poor Ernest slaves away, afraid he's going to lose his mother, afraid to ask questions, afraid of The General. I don't help him. And Olivia floats along, acting like she's having fun every day!"

"I can't believe all this."

"Oh really!" I blurted. "You think we're such a nice all-American family! You have no idea! Not even what's happening on your own street!" I drew back from him and wrapped my arms around my knees.

"Go on," he whispered as though I was telling some little story. As though *going on* weren't the whole big problem.

But I did go on. The moon was behind a cloud, so I couldn't even see Tom's face. Struggling to keep my voice down, I went on speaking into the stifling dark. "Daddy is always out of the house, saying it's some danged meeting, like the Republicans have a lot of pressing business on their agenda. What's wrong with Mama is she's got a husband running around on her!"

"You're saying your father has—" Tom sounded appalled.

"I don't know, maybe not. But I'm sure he's found someone who's very impressed with him."

When Tom didn't say anything, I hushed for a moment. "I guess I should say, it *looked* to me, as I was driving by, and saw him with this woman *for just a second,* to be a tender relationship. Affectionate. I'm sure. The problem is Mama can't get angry about it."

"Why not?"

"You're so naive, Tom." All the hot feelings gushed up again. "That Christian woman wouldn't dream of defending herself. She turns the other cheek. Fighting back would be unladylike! Women are supposed to be nice! Right, Tom?" I leaned forward and spat the words at him. "You have no idea! She tries to cajole Daddy like he's another child she's responsible for. Heaven knows he never sees himself. But mother, she can see it coming. She's nothing more than an old mop for his messes. And long after his flare-up's over and she's still smarting, he's completely forgotten the whole thing. And I'm going to be just like her—a little creep-around woman."

"Patty, not all men are like your daddy. Not all marriages have to be like your folks'. And sweetheart, you are not going to be a little creep-around woman."

"Oh, Tom!" I reached into the dark and put my arms around his neck. "More than anything! More than *anything*, I don't want to be like her." I hadn't thought of it this way before, but now it was out there, spoken aloud. My throat ached. "We've been afraid of him so long. It's a big relief when he's out of the house. It just never lasts long enough for Mother to find where she left her old self. Or for Ernest to get his head up. No wonder Mother's decided to lie down and leave it all to God."

Tom held me as I gasped and shook, his right arm pressing me to his chest; his left hand stuck between us to cup my mouth as though he expected me to scream. It might have been a good time for tears, but none came.

∾ ∽

All the next day I sat in my corner of the living room and barely went into Mama's room. I could hardly face her, knowing I had exposed her wretchedness to someone outside the family, especially to someone whose good opinion she wanted. More terrible than having sex when not married was violating family secrecy. Before last night, I'd felt grown up, brave and powerful. Now I was reduced to a guilty six-year-old. I'd thrown away a lifetime-perfect record of keeping my own counsel. The pattern, engraved since childhood, of confessing and taking my medicine seemed the only path to relieve the guilt. I listened all day to the smack of Ernest's hammer, nailing the walls onto his canoe. Finally, by nightfall, I knew what I had to do.

Around midnight I stood in the dark living room and watched the motorcycle cruise silently up under the elm trees. Every time before I'd watched for him with such longing, but tonight the sight of him washed a wave of nausea over me. I forced myself to walk out onto the porch and down the front walk. As I drew closer and could see his white shirt, the sleeves turned up on his beautiful forearms, I gritted my teeth. "I can't come," I said.

"Aw. Well." He looked down at the handlebars of the cycle, then glanced up, squinting. "Everything okay?"

"No. I mean, everything's fine." I stared at him, wishing he would do all this for me. Nothing was fine. If I confessed to Mother that I'd talked about her, she would say that I'd told information that wasn't mine to tell. I absolutely could not stand to hear that from her. I had to straighten this out on my own. "Everything's fine, Tom," I whispered.

"There isn't anybody leaning on you, is there?" He reached across the cycle and drew a finger lightly down my arm. "Is there?" His touch, so gentle and yet magnetic. I teetered, wanting to fall into him, to let him carry me away. His white shirt was open at the collar as usual—the little cup of his collarbone where I'd seen the sweat pool—"Patty?" he whispered.

"No. This is my decision."

He turned his head to the side to peer up into my downcast eyes. "Are you saying, goodbye, Patticake?" His face was white.

I walked back into the house. It would go easier on him in the long run to think I was cruel.

~~

I wouldn't go to the phone when he called, and I slid the little notes he delivered to the house, unread, between the pages of the books on my shelf. I didn't go to church for weeks, and when I finally did see him across the sanctuary, I tried to duck away. But he caught up with me as I reached the car. The glare of the noon sun was so great, I didn't lift my eyes from the tarmac and stood, my hand reaching toward the door handle which was too hot to touch.

"How's your mom?"

"Fine, thanks."

"That's great. Do you think she'd let me take you to a movie?"

"I'm kind of busy." I shouldn't have looked up at his sad face.

"Are you sorry we talked about your family? 'Cause surely that was long overdue."

I didn't say anything, just tried to look impatient, so he'd go before Ernest and Olivia and The General gathered around.

"I moved too slow, didn't I," he said. "Shoulda bought a ring."

A ring? I didn't deserve a ring.

"Now you're letting some other guy tell you jokes.

"No, Tom. Nobody tells jokes like you."

~

Early one morning in the middle of August, the grass in the backyard still wet, the canoe came out of the storage room. Mother, wearing moss green pedal pushers and her best Ship 'n Shore blouse, sat in a lawn chair in the dappled shade of a peach tree. Tonight we would all sleep deeply as the breeze swooshed through our open windows, sucked in by the giant fan that would be installed into this big hole under the eave. Daddy stood back in the storage room at the far end of the canoe, and we stood in the yard, watching while he slowly angled the huge canoe downward through the cut out toward Ernest's reaching hands. My brother's skinny legs swerved as he accepted the growing weight. Daddy held onto the top and walked toward the edge as Ernest staggered backward. He looked over his shoulder, and Olivia and I rushed forward to grab hold of the gunnels on either side, so that Daddy, now squatting in the eave, could let go. Amazing, that a twelve-year-old could build anything this heavy.

Ernest had set up sawhorses in the carport, and we laid the upturned canoe across them ready to be fitted with its canvas skin. Daddy and Ernest kept glancing timidly at each other, both grinning. Mother joined us beside the canoe, her arm around Ernest. She was the only one who knew how to stretch the canvas on the bias so it would hug the surface, and it seemed a miracle that she was standing here, ready and able.

~

"If I went to see a psychiatrist, would he make me tell him everything?" Mother asked me the next morning at the breakfast table as The General pulled out of the driveway.

"I don't know," I said. "But I think this is the thing to do."

"Not one of those at the University. Everyone says they're insane." She pressed her hands to her cheeks. "And not anyone out at the state hospital."

"Of course not." The state hospital had been a forbidden subject. Years ago she reported having watched a family try to keep an insane person at home. "It made no sense," she had said, and went on to emphasize that she certainly hoped her own family would plop her right into the state hospital if the need arose. But this summer she had remembered saying this and had reached up from her bed to take both my hands and beg me not to take her there.

This morning she tightened her lips and stared at the linoleum. "My grandmother was once in a mental hospital," she said.

"What grandmother?"

"Olivia Jane," she murmured. "They said it was terrible for her."

My great grandmother Olivia Jane?

∾ ∾

A week later Mother and I sat in the car and stared at Dr. David Mendler's clinic—six windowless walls joined at oblique angles, an acorn cap roof. Hovering atop a hill, like a flying saucer on one of the few promontories north of Oklahoma City, this place didn't look like a doctor's office.

"Do you want me to go in with you?"

"No, I should go alone." She looked around to see if anyone was watching, then pulled on the car door handle and struggled out into the wind. One hand holding her hair and the hard shell of her plastic summer purse banging from her elbow, she walked toward the entrance. She needed both her hands to pull open the massive door and squeeze inside.

Dust swept up from new flowerbeds and swirled around the foundation of the building. I hoped from the bottom of my heart that she would pour out everything. She could begin by telling how family happiness collapsed the day Daddy's letter came.

~

I was five years old when Daddy's letter told us he was finished occupying Japan and would be coming home. Mama laid down the letter and started cleaning up. She pulled all the leaves from around the rose bushes and loosened the dirt. I remembered, her curved spade made little scalloped edges next to the grass. Then she mowed the lawn and bought new garbage cans. Uncle Harold came home. My aunt and cousins packed up and moved. It was over.

Mama came down with a case of hives right after Daddy arrived. "Swelled up like a toad," he said. The doctor gave her some large blue pills, and she slept. Suddenly Daddy was in charge of me and Olivia.

First he inspected the house, not just our rooms, but under the beds and inside drawers and chests. A drawer that wasn't neat was dumped onto the bed. None of the closets passed inspection. Then he went outside to inspect the yard and the garage. He said he would organize the garage while Olivia and I shaped up our chest of drawers.

I got my collection of crepe paper streamers rolled up and nearly all my feathers back into the cigar box. But our costumes—feather hats and beads, old slips, the hoop skirt, and the cat outfit with the huge stripped tail Mama had sewn a wire in—just wouldn't go back in the drawer. I had to hide some stuff in the hamper and the washing machine before he came back to re-inspect.

Next Daddy crawled under the house—a space between the floor and the dirt hardly high enough for a dog to stand in. When he came out, he told Mother the house her grandfather had built wasn't level.

"How level does it have to be?" she asked sleepily.

"Level," he said. The next day he brought home some huge iron screws he called house jacks and crawled back under the house dragging these heavy things behind him into the little opening in the foundation.

When he crawled out to have a cigarette, cobwebs and fuzzy dirt hung from his curls, his army-colored undershirt was wet and stuck to the dark hair on his chest, and his shoulders were scraped and splintered. He looked so scary I ran inside.

One of the many beautiful things he brought back from Japan was a cigarette set: a silver lidded box and a smaller one for the matches sitting on a silver-rimmed ebony tray. "Farewell gift from my little Japanese house girl," he said to me. Mother looked right at me like *I'd* done something wrong.

As soon as her swelling from the hives had gone down, Mother repainted the kitchen woodwork white, but the roses stayed because the wallpaper was too expensive to rip off. She threw up everyday and said it was the paint. I made sure not to mention the house girl to Mother, but we didn't talk much anyway like we had when Daddy was in the war, and she never asked my opinion anymore.

At night I lay awake, noticing how our house sounded. The clicking of Fluffy's toe nails on the linoleum was gone, of course, but now the house itself made a kind of wheeze every once in a while like it was remembering the time before it was level. In her little bed Livvie cried out from bad dreams. I loved my little Livvie like part of my own body, and I wondered why Mama didn't come to her. Daddy liked to be the one to check on Livvie, to settle her down and shush her. He liked Livvie better than me. He never shushed me. Sometimes I stood by my parent's door and listened, but they never joked around like Mother and I used to at bedtime, and I knew she was lonely for me.

One Saturday afternoon Mama invited me to go on a walk with her on the campus. We sat down in the sunken garden beside a bed of marigolds and big red cannas. "Our family's been having a little trouble getting used to each other, haven't we?" she said.

I didn't know what she meant because our family was doing fine until Daddy butted in. "I just wish Aunt Fel and Harold and Sukie would come back."

"Sometimes Daddy—" she started, but she looked off into the marigolds. "We have to understand," she said, "that he was living in a conquered foreign land where an American army officer was like—. Well I don't know what they were like, but everyone did what they said. I guess," she went on, "it's best just to bury things and go on. Don't you think?" She looked right at me. I hadn't been ready for a question, but I nodded.

"You see, I have some wonderful news," Mama said. "It's going to make you more important than ever to me."

My heart fluttered. "You're going to have more responsibilities," she continued and picked up both my hands, "because God is sending us a new baby next March. I'm going to be counting on you."

In the morning before anyone else got up, I tiptoed out to the backyard in my pajamas, carrying the cigarette set. The sky was heavy purple and the grass was wet. I set down the black tray and crawled around in the sandpile until I found my shovel. Then I went over to the loose dirt Mama had dug up around the rose bushes and made a little hole and buried the match holder. I dragged my bare foot across the dirt to hide the spot. That was easy. I had to make a much bigger hole for the cigarette box, but I kept running into roots and catching my knuckles on the thorns. I gave up on a couple of spots before I got a big enough hole for the box. I squeezed it in and pressed my heel to force it down so I could cover it up.

"What do you think you're doin'?" It was Daddy in his army underwear. He grabbed me by the shoulder and yanked me away from my work. A little corner of the silver box showed, and the tray sat there on the grass. "That was given to *me!*" he yelled, and on his knees he dug in the dirt, hard and fast, like the boxes would smother.

I ran from his swinging hand, round and round, but he held my wrist up high, so he never missed. Then he went in and spread the cigarette set out on the kitchen table, still caked with dirt, and woke Mother up to come see what I had done. She cried and said she was sure I hadn't meant any disrespect. He made me stay at the table while he carefully cleaned the cigarette set with wads of cotton. "There are marks here," he said, "that will never go away." Then he got out the silver cream and polished 'til it hurt my eyes to look.

~

Mama seemed to have a tiny bit more strength when she returned to the car from meeting with Dr. Mendler. I asked nothing, just gently backed the Buick out and guided it down the hill to head back to Chisholm.

Finally, when we'd gone a mile or two, I asked, "What was it like?"

"Oh!" Her hands rose and fell into her lap, exhausted with the very thought. "This huge orange chair kept sliding me backward. I got so weary, my back hurts from leaning forward just to stay upright and keep my knees covered."

"I mean the doctor. What'd he say?"

"He said I wasn't crazy."

"That sounds helpful. When's your next appointment?"

"Friday at 2:00."

Yes! I told myself as I drove us back to Chisholm, now that I've helped Mama onto the path to recovery, maybe it's okay if I get Tom back!

~

The first time I called Tom's old boarding house I got a guy who was moving out after the summer session had closed. "This is Patricia Brady. I just wanted to ask if anyone there had heard from Tom Delaney."

"I heard he's gone out West—Spokane maybe or Portland. There's nobody else here right now." The next time I called a guy's voice said he'd never heard of Tom Delaney. I leaned on the kitchen table, my whole body cold. What if I'd lost him?

In a panic I ran to my bedroom and pulled Tom's notes from between the books on the shelf in my headboard. Why, why, why hadn't I read these when they came? I slit the envelopes and lay the notes on my bed. There was no return address. I really had believed that when he wasn't around for a while, my desire would fade, and I'd be quiet again about boys the way I had been before I met him. But he'd planted something in me as undeniable as a baby, and now I had to have him back.

> *There isn't a thing in this world that happened between us or ever will happen that you and I can't handle if you will just let us talk it out. Don't punish me. Don't punish yourself, Patticake.*

The first three notes repeated similar thoughts, but the next four sounded more urgent:

> *Please take the phone when I call. Call me back. Call me. I'm a man on a desert, sweetheart. Hurry!*

The last one, signed, "Love, Tom," like all the others, shook in my hand as I read and reread it.

> *Have I overestimated your iron resolve? Are you on the verge of returning to me? Should I stop the daily attempts to flog to death my love for you?*

I dressed carefully in a navy straight skirt and round collared blouse and worked on my courage to face Mrs. Runyon, the landlady Tom and I had started fooling in early spring.

Her living room was dim and crowded with ancient overstuffed furniture. I sat primly on the edge of a horsehair chair and pressed my knees together.

"Of course, Patricia Brady!" She said she recognized me from church, but I was pretty sure she was a Baptist. I told her I'd misplaced Tom's address.

"That Tom, such a wonderful young man, a real Christian gentleman." Mrs. Runyon's drapey flesh quivered around her chin. "Gone out West, that dickens."

I nodded. "Are you forwarding his mail?" I asked.

"With a situation like that, of course, he didn't know his address yet."

I nodded as though I knew exactly what she meant.

"I hope he gets the job, but I sure am gonna miss him. Mohammed might know something. Would you like me to ask?"

"Yes, please."

She pushed herself up from the couch and went into the hallway. She was nice, trusting. Here I was, posing as a good, church-going girl whereas even at this moment, smelling the familiar musty odor of this house, I wanted to be upstairs in the dark, moving on the patchwork quilt, sealed with sweat to Tom.

Mohammed stood in the hallway door. Mrs. Runyon was still working her way down the creaking stairs.

"Patricia," he said. He had on a dazzlingly white shirt, the creases showing from the package. Dark circles around his handsome eyes made him look like Omar Sharif. A slight Libyan, maybe thirty years old, he looked tenderly at me. There were hundred of Arabs on campus, but Mohammed was the only one I'd ever talked to.

Mrs. Runyon crowded past him and took up her place on the couch. "Sit down, Mohammed," she said, "Miss Brady wants to ask you about Tom Delaney." Her voice was raised, to make herself clear to the foreigner. I waited. Mohammed did not sit down. He took a couple of steps closer to me, and I thought he had something private to say. Vigilant in her chaperoning, Mrs. Runyon pulled a little forward on the couch. For the first time I saw Mohammed held an index card in his fine, caramel fingers.

"Tom thought you would come for this sooner," he said. "It may not be correct any longer." He looked so grave. I was sure he would have told me how much Tom loved me if Mrs. Runyon hadn't been sitting there.

It was the first Friday in September, and I was waiting for Mama outside the clinic in Oklahoma City. When she came out of the heavy door, I knew she had an announcement. A week ago she'd reported that Dr. Mendler had told her she had to start driving herself, so I thought she was about to tell me this was the last time I had to come to the clinic.

She repaired the wind damage to her hair and smoothed her skirt as I guided the Buick down the hill. "I need to find a job," she said, "because I'm going to seek a divorce from Cecil Brady."

We were whipping along pretty fast, the wind through the open windows making enough noise for me to doubt I'd heard her right.

"Go on," I said in the neutral tone she'd told me Dr. Mendler used.

"Don't you think I should?" She sounded like I'd objected.

"I'll help you, Mama. We'll get you a job and a divorce."

~

When I got home from registering for my sophomore classes, I found Mama sitting at the kitchen table writing on a white school tablet. She looked up like she'd been apprehended in a crime, then she squared her shoulders and said, "I'd appreciate it if you'd look this over, Patricia. I'm just trying to get my thoughts straight."

I picked up the tablet. "Why I Need a Divorce." with subtitles, Dignity, Fairness, Honesty, Trust.

"This is good, Mama, to get your thoughts straight, but a lawyer will need other arguments."

She didn't say anything, but the next day she cleaned out her closet and made repairs to everything that could be considered office wear. She read the want ads and made phone calls. She wasn't quite herself anymore. This new person had appointments to keep, forms to fill out, a ballpoint pen and a calendar in her purse.

"You're right to get a job lined up before you discuss anything with Daddy."

"I don't see how I can do this, Patricia, go off and leave you children. What about poor Ernest?"

"I'll look after Ernest. Don't think about leaving right now. Just think about getting a job."

"Daddy never wanted me to work after we got married."

"Mama!" I yelled. "Just get a job!"

The next day Mother was offered two jobs, one at the Chamber of Commerce, the other at the water company. She had come home shaking. "Congratulations," I whispered as I put on an apron to help her in the kitchen. She was making a roast beef and a chocolate cake.

"I've got to tell Daddy tonight," she said.

"Just about the job, right?"

"About everything. I feel so guilty plotting all the time. It isn't fair to him."

"Mother!" I said in a loud whisper. "You need to talk to a lawyer *before* you mention divorce to him. He will rattle you."

"I don't want a lawyer. I don't want a fight." She was stirring the gravy, hard, more like beating egg whites.

"Is there someone you could talk to, someone who's gotten a divorce? Maybe Clarice Windom's mother."

"I could never talk to *her*!" Mother's eyes looked frantic and she continued whipping the gravy. "Maybe you could ask Tom what we should do."

"Tom hasn't written me back yet. He went out to Washington State to a job interview."

"Why so far away when lots of law firms right here in town would be happy to have him?"

"You know, Mama, that's a very good question!" This came out from between my clenched teeth. "I let Tom go."

"Why?" she gasped. "Tom was wonderful. I thought he might be the one."

"Oh, no, Mama," I blurted. "I couldn't let myself go after a man that was good and whole. No. None of that for the women in this family! We ruin our own happiness!" I was hurting her, just as she was getting stronger, I was attacking, but I couldn't stop. "Why is that? Mama? Why is that?"

The meal should have been festive, but since three people at the table had no idea why we were eating like Christmas, conversation was stymied. Everyone said how good everything tasted, and Mama said three times how the meat had been on sale. Then we just ate. The General kept drawing himself up at the head of the table, his chest swelling beneath his tie, his eyes circling from me to Mama to Olivia to Ernest to the roast on his plate, looking for a clue.

After supper Olivia left for a friend's house, and I asked Ernest to help me with the dishes. He seemed relieved to have someone speak to him. It was only 7:00 o'clock, still light but over 90 degrees outside, so I told Ernest to get the attic fan going. I figured its roar and my steady stream of questions regarding his thoughts about going into the seventh grade would cover any surprise announcements that might be made elsewhere in the house.

Just as I was snapping closed the dishwasher there was a crash from the front bedroom and a shout from Mama. Ernest and I ran in to see The General on the floor and Mother bending over him. One of the china dresser lamps was smashed on the floor. She'd taken a shortcut to freedom, I figured, and killed him.

"Call an ambulance," she said. Ernest had already picked up the receiver.

~

"He's going to be okay," I said and patted Mother's hand. She'd sat down in the hallway for the first time since we'd arrived at the hospital, her in the ambulance with Daddy, and me and Ernest in the Buick. It was now nearly 3:00 a.m. Her pink shirtwaist was limp, its starched collar smudged from The General's resting head. "And you're going to be okay, too." I looked her straight in the eye.

"Oh, I couldn't go now. If ever God sent a sign, this was it."

"No!" I wailed. "You're wrong. A heart attack is not a sign from God. Why'd you tell him?"

"I had to tell him I wanted to leave. He had asked me why on earth I wanted to get a job. I've been impatient. God will show me how to be a better wife."

"Mama, please don't talk like that."

"Patty, darlin'." She looked across the hall to the name plate on my father's room, CECIL BRADY. "This is my job."

~

Three days later I brought the Buick to the hospital's discharge entrance and went up to my father's room. Olivia, her eyes focused on the ceiling, stood in the hallway holding a large gardenia plant. The General sat in a chair beside the bed, his hands in his lap, palms up. Mother moved about him like an old retainer, tying his shoes, buttoning his collar, intent on her job. Finished, she lifted her voice. "Patty, you and Ernest bring everything from the night stand." She sounded upbeat, in charge. "This wonderful nurse here will push Daddy's chair."

The General sagged between the supporting arms of mother and the nurse as they helped him toward the wheelchair. Tests had shown he hadn't had a heart attack, after all, but was suffering from high blood pressure. He sank heavily into the chair, chest bowed toward his belly, as if not daring to show any sign of health. I gritted my teeth and turned away toward the potted plants on the nightstand.

~ ~

Back home Olivia and Mother, each with an arm around his waist, helped The General into the house. Ernest offered to unload the plants from the car, but I said I'd do it. I placed the three delicate philodendron in the sun, pinched the buds off the gardenia, and gave the cactus a long drink from the hose. Ernest watched, a frown on his face.

"I don't get it," he said.

I looked up. "What don't you get, Ernest?"

He stared at the house where our parents' voices had faded as they'd made their way to the bedroom. "Them," he said. "I don't get them."

"Come on," I said and slung my arm across his shoulders. "Let's sit out in the orchard, so we can talk."

THE END

THE WOODPECKER
1934

So Patricia took her younger brother, Ernest, into the orchard, and with the intention of explaining why their mother agreed to marry their father, she found herself recounting fragments of a late night scene on a country road, details her mother had intentionally told Patricia before she was old enough to understand, details Patricia only began to comprehend as she remembered her mother's story.

Ever since Alice told her mother she loved Cecil Brady, the poor woman had been a little breathy in his presence. These tentative flutterings confused Cecil who also didn't know how to take her father's gentle abuse. "Now Cecil," Daddy had said on Sunday, "if you make your shoes any shinier, the ladies will have to carry parasols just to protect themselves from the glare."

Cecil told her privately he couldn't understand anyone who would make light of a guy's trying to put his best foot forward especially seeing as the country was in an economic depression—men standing in bread lines, Communists inciting strikes. On the other hand, Dan Hale, her father, could not resist teasing someone who regarded efficiency and ingenuity as cardinal virtues. She thought Cecil half-liked it that Daddy wasn't a good provider. Last night he'd asked, "Would it help if I paid the grocery bill after we married? Maybe you and I could take over the upstairs in exchange."

The idea had taken her breath away. It would solve everything. When he wasn't studying, Cecil could make all the household repairs Mother was always needing. And Daddy could stop selling off an acre here and there, willy-nilly to pay the taxes.

~

In her lap Alice adjusted the small box of jams and relishes she was bringing to Cecil's mother, the labels decorated with flourishes from her own mother's watercolor brush. If they continued to average thirty miles an hour in this ancient Ford, they'd be at his parents' house near McAlister in time for dinner at twelve. It would have been fun if she and Cecil had this Sunday to themselves and could drive down a country road and smooch. He was a catch—a fraternity boy with dark curly hair and a square jaw. He wasn't big, but he was aggressive—hadn't stood in the stag line with his hands in his pockets at that first *thé dansant*—had cut in and maneuvered her to a corner where other men couldn't see her. But there was no time to cuddle today. The sun was coming up, and there was work to be done.

Meeting his parents and two sisters for the first time was a task calling for all a lady's good manners. She ran her fingers over her hair, checking for any strays from the large knot at her nape, assessing the softness she'd arranged around her face. Her fingers were cold, and she slipped on her kid gloves. Cecil loved all this finery and that she read poetry on the campus radio station. His mother and sisters were undoubtedly very particular people.

But this morning Cecil hadn't said a word since they'd left her parents waving on the porch, and she could see his jaw working, that little throb that meant he was clenching his teeth. But he needn't pout, the two of them could handle this dinner if she could just shoo away his foul mood.

"I'm fully prepared for your sisters' resentment," she said gaily.

"Why would they resent you?"

"Because you are the youngest and their only brother, and they must adore you more than any breathing creature, which is only natural for older sisters who think no woman in the world is good enough for their smart, handsome, darling little brother."

Cecil snorted as though he'd never heard the like. "You're the one who wouldn't wear my pin until you'd met them."

"Well that was only proper. I certainly hope this is all right."

"It's all set up now." He said flatly. "It was your idea. Not mine."

∾ ∾

The house was not the mansion she'd pictured from Cecil's description. A large, plain clapboard painted a dark yellow with windows trimmed in brown, it had a long porch across the front and four wide steps leading up. But surrounding the house were all the trees he'd promised, bending over the roof in a nice protective way, waving up the hillsides behind the house—evergreens and broad leafs, tall and lush, their leaves turning red and yellow, so different from the stunted scrub oaks she'd grown up with.

The air was sweet and moist. And she could hear birds, perhaps the cardinals and blue birds and woodpeckers she'd seen only in books, solitary birds who sang alone, not flocking with a crowd. She stopped on the path to the door and listened, wishing she knew their separate voices or could hear a woodpecker tapping on a tree. "Come on," Cecil said, "and remember, you're my girl, and I love you, and you look like a million bucks." He took her hand and kissed her knuckles, then paused a moment to look at the house himself before leading her up the steps.

The wide front hall was impressive with yellow oak paneled walls and built-in benches on either side where she imagined men had waited to do business with the original owner, a cotton factor. These benches and the paneling would be something she could tell Mother about, but the house looked bare, and their footsteps echoed. Her heart thumped as Cecil's mother, Esther Brady, straight and trim, came down the stairs.

"Mother, this is Alice."

Mrs. Brady stuck out her hand and her eyes zipped up and down Alice's outfit. "How do you do." Alice handed her the box of preserves. "Thank you, Alice." Mrs. Brady turned to her son. "Did ya have any car trouble?"

This? Only this for the girl to whom her son had offered his fraternity pin? No welcoming hug? Where were his father and the two sisters?

"Y'all can sit in the living room." Mrs. Brady turned toward the back of the house. She must have hired help to speak to in the kitchen. Alice's fingers checked her hair.

~ ~

At dinner Alice carefully cut her fried chicken off the bone with her knife and fork and kept smiling. Elinor, the older of his sisters, sat across the table beside Cecil and dominated the conversation with talk of her own friends. She wore a lovely green silk with a shawl collar and a pearl necklace. She was a senior at O.U., very self-assured, handsome not beautiful, Alice thought, and intimidating. The middle child, Estelle, a junior, sat in silence beside Alice. This was the beauty, dark bobbed curls falling toward her round gray eyes. Perfect figure, perfect hands. She wore a high-necked lace blouse of the sort her mother might have worn as a girl. Engaged to a graduate student, a promising mathematician, her future was assured. Alice had seen her once on campus laughing with her sorority sisters.

Always laughing, those sorority girls, tossing their heads, floating in that other world where there were no concerns that couldn't be handled by a quick vote in a chapter meeting. When she'd stepped up on the porch, Alice had felt perfect in her copy of the designer suit, but now sitting next to the beautiful Estelle and across from the haughty Elinor, she suddenly felt home-made-with-loving-hands, the worst description a girl could receive on campus. Alice's mother had worked all day yesterday cutting, basting, fitting, between visits from her china-painting students. Then she'd worked all night doing the finishing work, using the lining from her own dressing gown to make the satin cuffs and collar. The sight of the dear old dressing gown, dismembered, and lying on the sofa with pages torn from the New York fashion magazine, had made Alice squeamish.

"Do you know any Phi Delts?" Elinor suddenly asked Alice. "Don't you think they're fun?"

"I might. I don't know," she said to Elinor. "I mean I don't know if I know any." She wished Cecil would help her out—tell his sister that she didn't care what fraternity a guy was in. But Cecil was busy shoveling the food into his mouth in the same noisy way he had when he'd eaten dinner with her parents. The girls sat with their hands in her laps, eating like little ladies. Why hadn't Cecil been taught better manners?

"Which house are you?" Estelle asked.

"I never got around to going through rush." Heat rose in her face.

"I told you," Elinor said to Estelle.

"Oh, of course. Sorry," Estelle said. "Cecil did say something."

She shouldn't have let herself sound disdainful. She should have said she was considering pledging as an upperclassman. Cecil was staring at his plate. Alice glanced upward. The ceiling fan was turning slowly over the table, but no breeze penetrated the heat pouring off her. If only she could start over, come in the front door again.

"We're Gamma Phi Beta's."

"I know," Alice said. She looked in her lap. Oh for heaven's sake! Mother had missed removing a row of tailor tacking along the edge of one of the cuffs. Under the table she began to pull at the thread. Why didn't Mrs. Brady change the subject? The woman seemed bent on tearing the flesh off that chicken back she held in front of her face.

"Yeah, cost me a fortune, those house fees," Mr. Brady said. He leaned back in his armchair, a broad-shouldered man with silver hair worn long and combed back. In his white linen Sunday suit, he looked twice the size of his son. "I left school after the sixth grade, myself. Our generation didn't put such emphasis on education," he said.

Alice smiled. She shouldn't mention she was the third generation of her family to go to college. "Your generation were men of action, right, Mr. Brady? My grandfather was an aide to Col. Joshua Chamberlain."

"He was a Yankee?" Mrs. Brady looked aghast. "All our people came from Mississippi."

"My mother's originally from North Carolina," Alice rushed to say. "My father was from Nebraska."

"What a marriage!" Elinor hooted.

"Oh, no. They don't care about the Civil War. It was so long ago."

"Did your father serve in the Great War?" Mrs. Brady asked.

"He tried, but he was too small."

"Then you're used to short stuff," Elinor laughed.

Incredible, an older sister making such an unkind remark. Poor Cecil. She should say something. But what could she say that wouldn't embarrass him? He was small, like her own father, but he had ten times Daddy's get up and go. Cecil would never let his family get in such straits as hers was in. But why didn't he help her right now with his own family? Was she the only one here who was trying to be nice?

And what was this table setting about? The napkins were damask and the plates Haviland, but the silver was all mismatched, some losing its plate. Her own family had no silver, nor much fine china either since all her mother painted went for barter or to pay the doctor bills, but she'd expected better of Cecil's family after all he'd told her. She looked at the handle of her fork.

"This is not our best silver," Mrs. Brady said. Mortified, Alice blushed and put down the fork. Mr. Brady snickered.

"I lost the silver," he said, leaning toward her, his dark hand cupped as though whispering a secret, "playing cards one night down at the Odd Fellows Hall. Woulda claimed the other guy was cheatin' but he had a gun."

Elinor shot her father a dark look. Estelle sighed. Mr. Brady slapped the corner of the table next to Alice, and she jumped. "Know what's good for business, Alice?" he said just to her. "Last Saturday I found out what's good for business. A body. Yes, sir. Even better, a murdered body."

"C.L.," Mrs. Brady murmured, but Mr. Brady went right on.

"A murdered body on a wagon was driven up right in front of Mingles."

"I showed you Mingles Drug," Cecil said, "when we came through the downtown."

"Yes, yes, I remember."

"You know, Alice, I learned all about business when I clerked for J.J. McAlister, himself." Mr. Brady leaned closer. "Now about this body. You see, Alice, Dr. Harris hangs out in the drug store at one of the back tables of the ice cream parlor. A family can't bury a body without a death certificate from him, and if the death's from natural causes, the doctor just signs a certificate and sends the body on to Chaney's. But this body had been shot right in the heart. A big guy with whiskers. I was standing in the window of my store and could see the bloody shirt when Harris came out with his black bag to make his examination. Now since this was clearly a murder—"

"It could have been an accident," Cecil said.

"Shut up, Cecil," Mr. Brady said softly and continued.

Alice gasped, a father talking that way at the table. Cecil clenched his jaw and looked down.

"Since this was clearly a murder, *Alice—*" Mr. Brady emphasized her name, insisting she turn back to him—"Harris had to notify the county sheriff who is never around when you need him. So that corpse lay there in the sunshine all afternoon, drawing a huge crowd, plenty who came into my store. Even better for business than a good fight." He tossed his napkin across his plate.

Alice smiled back at her host. Did he like her? She was sure none of the others did. Cecil was again staring at his plate. He'd pointed out the store with pride, but admitted the boarded-up hotel was also his father's. She glanced around the dining room. There was a fine Seth Thomas clock on the mantle, but not much else. A dusty rectangle on the paint over the mantle suggested a missing painting or mirror. There was no silver service on a tea cart as she'd expected, no carpets. Had there been more nice possessions? Things they'd sold or pawned? But if they themselves were on hard times, why were they being so snippy to her?

"Business all over the country just gets worse and worse," Mr. Brady said.

"If you'd make your tenants pay their rent," Mrs. Brady said, "things would be a whole lot better." She rose and carried the chicken platter to the kitchen.

"Used to, Estelle and I each had blooded mares to ride when we were home," Elinor said.

"Blooded mares! How grand." Alice looked at the clock. 1:10. Dessert, a few pleasantries, and they could leave.

Mrs. Brady returned with a chess pie and served everyone a piece. "My, this is heavenly, Mrs. Brady," Alice said. Mrs. Brady shrugged.

"Your mother's a painter, isn't she?" Estelle asked. "It must be wonderful to live in a house full of paintings."

"Oh, we can't afford to keep them." Silence. Estelle and Elinor exchanged looks.

"Let's walk to the creek," Mr. Brady said to Alice.

"I was gonna drive her around," Cecil said, "show her Grand Avenue, all those homes."

"Naw, you don't want to do that," Mr. Brady said. "It's a beautiful day." Cecil glared at his father.

"You change your clothes," Mrs. Brady said to her husband. It was late in the season for a white suit, Alice realized. Mother always made Daddy put away his straw hat on Labor Day.

"A little walk beneath the trees would be lovely," Alice said. "Why, when my daddy's family first pioneered from Nebraska in the 1880's, there were so few trees, they first had to live in a dugout." The members of the family rose from the table without response. Perhaps relatives living in the ground like prairie dogs was not the best heritage to be claiming at this table.

~

Mr. Brady came downstairs in a tweed jacket and twill pants. He carried a rifle, and as he, Cecil and Alice rounded the house, he picked up a heavy looking gunny sack. "Do you shoot?" he asked her.

"Never have, no sir."

They walked through a backyard bordered by beds of day lilies. In the center of the yard was a statue of a little boy holding a big fish with a tube emerging from its mouth, but the small moat around the statue was dry. Cecil had told her they'd had parties here once, but today no guests had been invited to meet her.

The ground rose sharply once they were out of the yard, and Cecil took her hand as they climbed past a large outcropping of rock toward a grove of white-trunked trees. "Cottonwoods," Cecil said, "and those are hickories."

"Lovely," she said, looking up, then down, watching where she put each step to protect her shoes. A walk was actually not a great idea for her, traipsing through grass in pale suede pumps. Mother had traded a huge, lidded soup tureen, trimmed in gold to Mr. Welcher for these shoes. Mr. Brady took long strides, a man easy in his body.

At the top of the rise, she saw that the land plunged down toward a ribbon of dark water overhung by willows—lovely, like a scene Mother might paint on a platter. Cecil pulled her into a run toward the water leaving Mr. Brady to saunter down to the bank with the rifle and the gunny.

"You want a cigarette?" Cecil whispered when they reached the bank.

Yes, yes, that would really help, but she whispered, "Cecil, I wouldn't smoke a cigarette in front of your father."

He dropped her hand and fished his Lucky Strikes out of his pocket. He was the only one who knew she liked the taste of cigarettes, and she felt uneasy, not accepting his offer. To be alone with him, beside this rushing water, leaning her head back on a tree, exhaling a little plume of smoke from red lips—

Mr. Brady rested the rifle and the gunny sack against a tree, then sat down in the shade and took off his jacket. "Go on and swim, Cecil," he said, "I'll take care of Alice."

"It's October, Daddy. I'm not gonna swim." He sucked hard on his cigarette and flipped it toward the creek.

"Alice, come here and sit in the shade." Mr. Brady spread open his coat on the ground beside him, and she sat on it and pulled her feet under her skirt where she could slip her heels out of the shoes which had started to rub. A bird chirped, and she felt her shoulders relax. Cecil came and sat on the grass beside her. Mr. Brady took up his rifle, aimed toward a floating tree branch in the creek and fired. She clutched her waist, head down, ears ringing. Cecil put his arm around her.

"I'm sorry, Alice," Mr. Brady said, "I shoulda warned ya. I really am sorry."

"That's all right," she said. "I've just never been up close to a gun when it was fired, except at the pictures, of course." She smiled at Cecil.

"Now, Alice," Mr. Brady said, "the report won't shock so when you do it yourself. You'll see. Stand up." He handed her the rifle and stood to help her hold it properly. The gun was huge and awkward, and the smell of gunpowder was sharp in her nose. She willed her hands to stop shaking and bent her eye to line up the sights as she was instructed. If Cecil didn't want her to do this, he should speak up. But he didn't say anything, just stood up to get out of the way as his father moved around behind to adjust her elbows. "Now think of the trigger like it's a lemon you're squeezin'," Mr. Brady said close to her face. "Forget about pullin'. Use your whole hand. Just relax. Now line up the sights. See that big branch out there in the middle. Hit that."

She didn't wait to take a breath, but fired twice on command.

Mr. Brady grinned and pointed and spoke to Cecil who made a faint smile. She wanted to go now. She could not hear any birds or even the sound of the water rushing along.

She extended the gun to Mr. Brady and watched his lips moving. Her ears popped and her hearing returned. ". . . back to me. No, ma'am. You've got lots of shooting left to do." The gun was heavy, and holding it, she didn't feel like herself.

"Maybe Alice doesn't care for shooting," Cecil said.

She didn't, but it seemed to be Mr. Brady's planned entertainment for her. "Oh, I don't know," she said. "Maybe I'd better try to learn while I have the chance."

Mr. Brady fished two long bullets out of his pocket. Then his sun-splotched hands took the rifle from her and broke it open to show her where the bullets belonged. She took off her suit coat, folded it on Mr. Brady's opened jacket, and unbuttoned the cuffs of her silk blouse. He reached into the gunnysack, pulled out a dried corncob, and threw it way up the creek. It bobbed to the surface and floated along in the current toward them, a little boat alone. "Now take aim, careful, careful and fire."

She couldn't catch Cecil's eye.

"Go on, Alice, take aim," Mr. Brady said. By the time she spotted the corncob again, it had passed them in its ride. She lined up the two sights, pointed at the receding cob and fired. The cob shot up onto the far bank. She swallowed to clear her ears. "Awww right! Fine and dandy, Alice. You are an absolute natural sharp shooter. Did you see that, Cecil? Did you see that?"

But Cecil didn't answer, just stooped to pick up a stone and sailed it hard toward the broadest part of the water. She handed back the rifle. "I think Cecil's ready to go," she said.

"Naw," Cecil said, "Y'all go on. I think I'll just lie down right here after all that dinner." He lay back on the ground and rested his head on his folded arms. Didn't he care now if she went deaf pleasing his father?

"Come on now, Alice," Mr. Brady said. "This is too easy for you. Break open the rifle like I did." He handed her four more bullets. She dropped two into her skirt pocket, inserted the others into the holes in the rifle, and snapped it closed as she'd seen him do. He dug into the gunny, grabbing two cobs with each hand. "Now I'm going to throw them in one after another. You don't have to hit them in order, but pick your shots carefully."

She spread her legs to the limit of the slim skirt. The breeze stroked her hair back and pressed the skirt between her legs. Cecil watched. Perhaps she *was* good at this. Did Elinor and Estelle shoot? Was it part of the land-owning life? She could play this role, a redhead in a chamois skirt, her hair held at the nape in a black ribbon, a rifle at her side.

"Hold it," Mr. Brady said. He dropped the cobs and put his arms around hers. She didn't have it right. Whatever had been natural at first was lost now. "The way your doing, you're gonna throw out your shoulder." She could smell his sweat and heavy after-shave. His heat surrounded her, his leg firm against her hip. Her heart pounded. "Ease it down this way. That's a girl."

Suddenly, beside her on the ground Cecil cried, "Hit that," and pointed to the sky, then to a flutter of leaves on a tree behind her. She turned, aimed and fired. Something fell like a stone to the earth.

"You little bastard," Mr. Brady hissed.

He took the rifle, and she dashed to the base of the tree. She stooped down and saw the red cap on the bird's head. The first real woodpecker she'd ever seen. Why had she fired without knowing what it was? She blinked back tears and stood up. She wanted to go home. She hated this family. Why had Cecil done this to her?

Mr. Brady gathered up both their jackets, and with the rifle at his side, walked up the bank toward her. "Come on, Alice. It's starting to get chilly." He held her suit jacket by the nape, and she slid her arms in.

Cecil was nowhere to be seen. With shaking knees she slipped and slid in the high heels as she and Mr. Brady made their way up the rise. Mr. Brady tried to keep a hand under her elbow, but she was still sniffling and turned her head away so he couldn't see her face. Where was Cecil? She didn't know whether they were headed for the house or away. She was in no condition to face the women.

"Now just stop right there," Mr. Brady said softly. They were standing in a little clearing. Alice's heart thumped. "Someone wants to take your picture," he said.

What on earth? Alice looked about and finally, in the trees, saw the top of a dark head bending over a box camera, hair as long and dark as an Indian. Mr. Brady stepped away. Alice sniffed and wiped her cheeks. She patted her hair, but without a mirror, it was hopeless, so she just lifted her chin to the side and composed a model's smile.

"Did you get her?" Mr. Brady said and headed for the person with the camera. Alice shielded her eyes and looked into the deep shade. It was a small white woman with her hair down. The loose hair made her look like a girl, but Alice saw now that the woman's tan face showed the white squint marks of someone who'd worked in the sun for years.

She wore a dark dress and lace-up lady's shoes and held Mr. Brady's coat while he wound the film in the camera. "Come here, Alice," he said and waved her closer. The small woman turned to leave, but Mr. Brady said to her, "You might as well say hello." He lifted a branch aside and Alice stepped into the cool shade where the festering smell of the forest floor surrounded the three of them.

"Miss Sarah meet Miss Alice."

"Pleased to meet ya, Miss Alice," the woman said, nodding her head with meticulous country manners.

"How do you do," Alice said and smiled.

"Fine, thank you," Sarah said, clearly nervous. Mr. Brady put the little roll of film in his pants pocket, and Miss Sarah held up his jacket for him. Alice watched as he slid in his long arms and this woman smoothed her hands along his broad shoulders. He took Alice's elbow and walked her out again into the sun. She was going to have to think about all this later.

When they came in, Mrs. Brady was in the front hall. "You bring me anything?" she asked her husband.

"Couldn't hit the side of a barn," he said, and without a glance at Alice, headed upstairs.

"Cecil's in the kitchen talking to Estelle," Mrs. Brady said to Alice. " You can wait in the living room." Had Cecil told his mother about the woodpecker?

Alice sat down on the edge of a stuffed chair and looked at her ruined shoes—all Mother's work on the tureen gone in an afternoon. Her blouse was damp with perspiration. She ran her fingers over her hair, tucked up stray strands and tried to pat the sides into a decent shape. If she had had the money for a bus ticket, she would never get in a car with Cecil Brady again.

She clasped her hands now and waited for this horrible day to end. These people were Philistines, interested only in money and social position. Cecil loved to hang around the Drama building and help with the sets and the lighting. He was always telling people his girl was an actress or bragging about her reading poetry on the radio. She thought he valued all this as much as she did. But he didn't care about theater or poetry. And his sisters seemed to think she'd be a social embarrassment. This was the last family in the world in which she would ever feel comfortable.

"Are you two going back now or staying?" Mrs. Brady asked from the doorway. Alice sat there dumbfounded. How would her own mother have put that question? *"I hope you're not rushing way." Or, "Supper's almost ready. It would be such a treat if you'd stay a little longer."*

Behind his mother, Cecil dashed through the front hall with his hat on and a paper bag in his hand. Alice heard the front door slam.

"It seems we're leaving." Alice stood up. Elinor came down the stairs and Estelle came out of the kitchen.

"Looks like you ruined your shoes," Elinor said. "Too bad the hired girl isn't here today to clean them up."

"Oh, no, Daddy will do it." She blushed. Was there no opportunity she'd pass up to embarrass herself? She measured the distance to the front steps and felt Cecil's family closing in behind her as she walked into the late afternoon shadows. Cecil had started the car. She paused on the porch to make a proper farewell. "It was kind of you to have me, Mrs. Brady. The dinner was delicious."

"Glad you could come," Mrs. Brady said, her arms hanging at her sides.

Estelle, delicate and lovely, had come only as far as the threshold and stood framed by the brown doorway. "You're going to be driving in the dark."

For over thirty miles neither of them said anything. Alice's back ached from sitting up so straight. What was there to say? He'd misled her. At least, he'd certainly left out a lot and given her no warning at all about how cold his mother and sisters could be. No one mentioned her gift of the preserves with their water-colored labels. His family acted like she'd come empty handed. Kindness counted for nothing. Courtesy or generosity—all signs of weakness. Mother would be so disappointed.

"The Gamma Phi Betas won't rush you," Cecil said finally. "Elinor told me. It's completely out."

Her head snapped around. "Cecil! How did this come up? You said you didn't care if I wasn't in a sorority. I could never afford one anyway, and it's humiliating that you even discussed it with your sister."

"Elinor says, for a future in society, a person should have this valuable connection. She said you have the clothes and manners, but she says you don't know how to make the best of yourself."

"In what way is it that I do not make the best of myself?"

"Everything. You never mentioned that you're on the radio every week. Or that your grandmother went to college. You talked poor from the moment you walked in."

And you've talked big ever since I met you—all your father's holdings. Saying that would have stopped him, but she didn't say it aloud. Nor did she say, how can you, who talk with your mouth full at the table, say I do not present myself well? She stared through the dusk at the rolling tree-covered hills. In another hour they'd be back in the flat land.

"Look, Alice!" He sounded truly irritated. "I didn't want to take you out there. But you insisted. Now you're giving me the silent treatment."

The silent treatment was surely a whole lot better than the ugly bickering she'd heard at his folks' table. She'd be embarrassed to have her family see them. They had made her feel lonely, and she felt lonely now. The sun was going down, and she had so far to go with this angry man.

"God damn it!" Cecil yelled. "You didn't want this to go well. Every word out of your mouth—"

She raised her hand to hush him. She could not allow them to sink to this—yelling and cussing. Her parents never raised their voices in anger.

"You!" The word spurted out of his mouth. "You pass yourself off as too good for us. An artist who wouldn't think of socializing with sorority girls."

"Cecil, I never said that. I'd love to be in a sorority."

"Estelle says you're a phony."

"Estelle?" Alice wanted to get out of the car and walk the last hundred miles home. "How could anyone say that about me. We may not have a lot of land and a big house, but we—?"

"Wouldn't you like a big house, Alice?" He glanced over at her. "How about a real pearl necklace like Elinor's. I saw you staring at it. Huh? Be honest. You're crushed my family has fallen on hard times. You thought you were getting a rich boy. My daddy's thirty thousand dollars in debt. He's lost everything but the land and nobody will buy it from him. He's filed for bankruptcy on the mercantile. I drove out from Chisholm last month to bail him out of jail for fighting."

Her breath. She couldn't get her breath. Finally she said softly, "You didn't tell me any of this."

"Well you know now." He said this last with such a bitter stab she knew it was all ended, her romance with Cecil Brady was over. He was withdrawing the strong arms he'd offered. The car began to slow down. Was he about to dump her beside the road?

"God damn it!" Cecil said. The car bucked up onto the weedy shoulder beside a field of dried corn stalks. Cecil jumped out.

Against the very last purple light along the horizon he stood and wiped his hand down his mouth before folding open the hood of his old Ford. It served him right, this old car breaking down. But this was a bad spot. There wasn't a house in sight and they must be twenty miles yet from Ada which wasn't half way home. She pulled to the edge of her seat and watched his fingers checking the clamps on the hoses, tightening the cap on the radiator, and knew he wasn't working on the problem yet. This was just the fiddling he always did, calming his mind while he thought about the problem. Was the throttle stuck? That wouldn't be so bad. He could fix that.

He walked back and handed his jacket through the window without looking at her. It was getting dark now. She opened the glove compartment, took out the big flashlight, and quietly got out to come around behind him and shine the light where his hands were working.

"Higher!" he snapped, and she moved the light a fraction of an inch. His fingers were black up to the knuckles. He wasn't working on the throttle. This was something more serious. A car approached. Maybe they should flag it down for help, but it wasn't her place to suggest this. In another few hours Mother and Daddy would start to worry. The wind had come up and whipped the hem of her jacket and pressed her skirt against her legs. She should get Cecil's jacket from the car. He was sweating and could take a chill.

"Steady!" he barked and she switched hands with the flashlight and tried to breath lightly so the beam of the light came down steadily at just the right angle to cast the least shadows.

"Don't you have any tools in the car?" she asked as sweetly as she could. "Surely a few wrenches under the seat."

"It wouldn't make any difference. I need a spanner. Couldn't reach this with a wrench."

Maybe at a farmhouse down the road he could borrow a spanner. Maybe if he took the battery out he could reach down to whatever it was he needed to turn. Could her slim fingers reach down? Maybe they should find a house and telephone home to ask Daddy to come to get them. Cecil looked up and down the straight road. There wasn't a headlight coming in either direction. The wind was loud now, rattling the dry corn stalks. Where was the house of the farmer who'd strung this fence?

Cecil dropped his hands to his sides, and she switched off the flashlight. They were in total darkness. There was no moon, no stars, just Cecil's labored breathing beside her. She shook with the cold and felt a little faint. She'd eaten so little at dinner and then the long walk and the shooting. Cecil didn't care about her anymore; and the long black corridors between the corn stalks could hide any kind of danger. She felt the darkness choking her.

Cecil was the phony. His family had no money. This car she'd taken for an antique, his hobby, was just old, the only thing he could afford. His father was a gambler whose estate was in ruin. She wanted to scream with disappointment. The wind in the corn stalks sounded like bones rattling, and she wrapped her arms around her waist.

So Cecil was right about her. She did want a big house, one with radiators, a tight roof and a veranda, thank you very much. She wanted piles of silk stockings and heavy bond paper, a car that ran, and crystal that sang when you thumped it. Not having things at the moment didn't mean you weren't a materialist. She'd pretended she wanted an artist's life. But whoever heard of Bohemians in Oklahoma? Who was she kidding?

She wasn't even the lady she'd thought she was this morning before she felt C.L. Brady's leg against her hip, and realized she had a taste for recklessness. *And* a man like this, a gambler, a fighter, a big guy, one who clearly had a taste for her. It was in that distorted red moment, his body crouched around her, that she'd wheeled and aimed and killed the woodpecker.

Cecil rested his hands on the open hood. She could barely see them against the old car. Closing the hood had always been the sign of success; his triumphing over whatever difficulty the machine had presented him. His wonderful mechanical ability solved the kinds of problems that so confounded Daddy. But this time he didn't have the solution, and she knew his hands didn't want to fold out the cover and fasten it down until he'd licked the problem.

What were they going to do? She knew if he were alone he could sleep in the car until morning, then walk down the road easy as pie to borrow a spanner and fix the car and come home with a good story to tell—the joke on him for cleaning out the car, wanting it to be so neat as a pin, he forgot to put back the tools he always had lying under the seat.

But she *was* there, weakening him by witnessing his failure and adding a huge responsibility. Staying alone together, huddled in the car wasn't a possibility. Both families would be scandalized. He wouldn't go for help and leave her alone on this dark road, nor could he call her father to come get them and admit he wasn't capable of looking after her. She knew he'd rather slit his throat. She felt like a huge unwieldy package, a burden he no longer wanted. And she was shaking uncontrollably as the wind drove through the challis and the silk.

Cecil's hands still lay on the hood. Was he thinking of calling his father? Surely that was the answer. It would take a couple of hours, driving at night, for Mr. Brady to reach them, but he would come. He would come for *her,* the sure-shot, willowy college girl. She knew it. If Cecil had been alone, his father would have told him to hang on 'til morning, this small son who wouldn't gamble, who would never take the chances the high-rolling C.L. Brady had–*not the man his father was by a long shot.* That's what his father thought. She understood now, that sense of struggle for place she'd felt in Cecil–not the darling baby of the family he should have been, not worth a trip in the dark.

Swamped with a wave of pity for Cecil, she stepped up to his side and laid her head on his shoulder. He lifted his dirty hands, but dropped them back on the hood and laid his head against hers. He was warm, and she pressed herself against him.

They sat inside the car and Cecil wiped his hands on the rag from the glove box. The noisy wind drove into every seam of the old car. Cecil took his jacket and wrapped it around her. "I've got only one idea," he said, "and it's kind of dumb and probably won't work, but it's all I've got." In the dark she guessed he was looking at her, needing her permission or encouragement.

"Hey," she said, "Let's give her a try."

From behind the seat he took the brown paper bag he'd carried when he left his folks' place. He took out two apples then two large sandwiches wrapped in waxed paper. "Here," he said, "you eat now. I'll eat after we're rolling." He'd probably made these himself in the kitchen while she walked back with his father. He was thinking ahead, thinking of her. He kissed her. His lip was moist with sweat.

"To hell with them," he said. "To hell with all of them." Then he got out into the driving wind, and as he did, his flapping white shirt was illuminated by a shaft of moonlight as a cloud was swept aside. He looked up at the moon and then back to grin at her as though God had smiled on his cockamamie plan. He began to unwind a piece of wire from the fence post beside the cornfield. She watched as the wind blew his dark curls, and she saw him snap his hand back in pain then suck on one of his fingers for a moment before going back to twisting the wire off the post.

For the first time, she thought of the small woman who'd taken her picture in the woods—probably a tenant of Mr. Brady's, maybe one he wasn't collecting the rent from, someone who'd known Cecil since he was a boy and wanted a picture of his girl. For a split second the idea danced on the edge of her mind that the woman with the camera was Cecil's real mother. But she knew that outlandish thought presented itself because Sarah was the only woman to show her any respect. On the other hand that woman's rough hands had smoothed the shoulders of Mr. Brady's jacket—an undeniably intimate gesture. She looked at the top of Cecil's head as he leaned over the motor. She would never find out the whole story about Sarah because Cecil wouldn't know. He hadn't the kind of mind where outlandish thoughts danced. And a grand, creative mind was not what she needed anyway, not with her family in the shape it was in.

Now he was very carefully twisting the fence post wire around something in the motor. He would try anything; whereas her father, would try nothing. Mother would scrape and scavenge and work all night to make something possible for one of her children, but Daddy held back from life and things. He could drive a car, but if it balked, he walked away from it. Cecil took everything apart and put it back together. Daddy opened only books. What she needed was a go-getter who wouldn't let her down as Daddy did, sweetly, quietly, over and over. And a father who wanted to read all the time should have inherited money, instead of being a penniless scholar who refused to teach school.

Cecil would get this car cranked up and rolling within an hour and have her home before midnight. Mother would be up sketching in the dim light of the front room or perhaps sewing, putting her dressing gown back together with another lining borrowed from something even older. But most important she would be waiting, eager for a report of Alice's first visit with Cecil's family.

Thank heaven, Mother and Daddy hadn't been there, so she was free to set the scene for her parents–a thousand tree-covered acres and the image of the cotton factor in whose oak paneled entry hall clients had long ago waited. She'd talk of the ceiling fan cooling the long damask-covered dining table and the Haviland china, and the beautiful Estelle, about to make such a promising marriage. She would mention Cecil's father, how he struggled with his businesses, but rush on to tell of his gallantry toward her and discovering what a keen marksman she was. All the rest, she would forget—the missing silver, Miss Sarah, and the Gamma Phi Betas. And she would not mention Mrs. Brady's lack of warmth or that no one mentioned the challis suit. There was so much she would try to forget, especially that before Cecil had called to her, he had seen that woodpecker in full flight and had to have known it for what it was.

THE END

THE INVESTMENT IN LILLIAN GISH 1923

What did little Alice absorb as she listened at the door to her parents' conversations, what did she make of this marriage she knew intimately and didn't know at all?

"Think there's anything you could do with this, Mrs. Hale?" Mr. Greenbaum said as he heaved the bolt onto the counter. Victoria watched him roll it out and could tell from the dust and the faded edges he'd had it on the shelf for years. How long had he waited for a day when she was the only customer in his store, so no one would catch Victoria Hale being offered his stalest piece of goods? She knew he meant her well—a good customer, a seamstress others copied, the best milliner in town. She couldn't hide from him the hunger with which she waited for the remnants and sorted through his damaged goods. She had rubbed the wool jersey between her fingertips, soft and drapey. This would do.

Mr. Greenbaum had given her the bolt for six cents a yard and let her put it on the bill. She'd washed it, her hands turning bright red in the cold water, squeezed the suds through it, and rinsed it in two different tubs, twenty yards of the heavy, water-darkened wool.

"Now, Vic, what did you say you were going to do with this?" Dan laughed as he helped her wrestle it all onto the clothes lines, looping it back and forth like so many hammocks, miles of lank wool, pulling the lines low and causing the poles to lean toward each other so precipitously Dan had to drive stakes at the base of the poles, lest the wind come up and lash all her hard work about the yard.

When, after three winter days it was all dry, she cut off the faded selvage. The fading on the fold, little more than a milkier shade of the cream would be lost in the gathering. With the ironing board at the head of the dining table, she'd pressed and lapped and pressed and lapped, sending Alice and Felicity back to the kitchen to reheat the iron and dampen the pressing cloth while she rested in the window seat, sewing feathers on hats for Mrs. Woodbury and her daughter.

Dan, his sandy hair arcing over his fine freckled nose, had made tassels for her from fine string wrapped around one of his mother's little volumes of poetry, so they all came out alike. "These go on the tie backs, right?" he'd asked after proudly turning out a couple of dozen.

"No darlin', on the edges of each pair."

"Floor to ceiling edges? Vic, that'll take hundreds! I'm in the middle of Huxley's new book. At this rate, I won't get another word read 'til spring. Wouldn't you rather I read to you than just sitting here mindlessly wrapping up Keats in packing twine."

"You'll talk to me."

"Well, of course, but—"

"I've set my heart on this, Dan."

When the generously gathered draperies were tied back, the tassels hung with a delicate authority, framing the lilac bushes in the foreground, and then the prairie and the town of Chisholm in the distance. Every day the town prospered and the university and library grew and there were even moving pictures at the opera house. And when folks passed on the road or stopped to fish in the creek, she wanted them to see a gracious country home, not a farmhouse. She knew how to distract the eye from peeling paint with boxes of geraniums or petunias spilling from the porch railing. And inside, the soft light from a table lamp falling on a pile of books and bowl of pecans could create a sense of culture and leisure. She rested her fists on her hips and sighed. In another life she might have been supervising a team of painters and gardeners, a choice gone by.

It had been a breezy day at a town social in 1910 when she, a spinster of thirty, had chosen Dan Hale over Karl Winberg, the well-to-do baker. Long tables had been brought out onto the Mayor's lawn, covered with fluttering white tablecloths and heaped with pies and cakes. The boys had three large ice cream churns going; the girls took turns sitting on the gunny-sack-covered churns to hold in the ice. She'd stood at the edge of the lawn—a new hat with cascading pink rose buds fastened onto her piled up red hair—and taken in the flurry of the social. What a picture! If she were a real painter, this is what she'd paint: white dresses moving against the green grass; little willows in the side yard shaking sunlight on old ladies in rockers; farmers on the wide porch, one foot up on the railing, hats tipped back from pale foreheads taking their ease of a Sunday afternoon. And all of it laced together with running, skipping children.

Victoria smiled. Karl Winberg had been there, a man with a lot to offer, much of it light and sweet and packaged in the white boxes from his family's bakery. Last year he had stood on her father's porch holding the white boxes in chubby, outstretched hands—pastries, fragrant with cinnamon, apricot and apple. "Why, Karl, how nice," she said each time, taking the boxes.

His broad moist face reddened, his smile stretched his face painfully. "There's no lemon this time," he blurted.

"Ah well, the lemon was lovely. But these smell divine. Tell your mother—

"It's not that there's anything wrong with our lemon. It's just this time—" Mouth open, he patted the sides of his jacket probably drying his palms.

"Of course. Karl, I'd ask you in, but Father is napping."

Karl nodded vigorously, and stepped backward, doubtless eager to avoid the Judge. Now with his hands free, he whipped off his hat. "Sorry," he said.

"Oh no," she said. "Your hat was fine—"

"I'll go."

"—on the porch. Father and Wendell will be pleased with the pastries. They say there isn't another town in the Territory with such a bakery as Winberg's."

"We'll be a bona fide state soon. It's already 1906." Karl, having introduced a new topic, shifted his weight and clasped his hands.

"My yes, within a year, they say."

"Maybe less," he said

"Ah." She gave up on that and just smiled as he looked backward to keep from stepping off crooked, then put his hat on so he could doff it two or three times as he backed down the steps, still red and smiling. He'd been smart enough to let his mother take over the courtship after that.

Now, thirteen years after Karl Winberg's mother made her an indirect offer of marriage to her son, Victoria shook her head, wondering why that offer had plunged her into gloom. But today she smiled. The best part of that offer which included living in the finest house in town had been Mrs. Winberg herself.

One hand on the ironing board, Victoria pressed her other hand into her arched back. She and Dan had worked late last night. In the spring she would cut forsythia or apple branches to place in her blue lemonade pitcher in front of the bay's middle window, but even without flowers she was greatly satisfied with the effect. These draperies would never look new like the crisp organdy everyone else was putting up. Instead these looked grand and old and rich, like they'd been hanging there since her wedding.

Hearing little Alice's voice, she walked through the music room to look out just below the window where eight-year-old Alice lay in the yard, her head leaning against her sleeping white sow, Lillian Gish.

"Do you ever think about heaven, Lillian?" Victoria heard Alice ask her pig.

"I think about heaven all the time. Mother says whenif—that's her word, whenif—whenif she gets to heaven, all the boys and girls will wear black, so the berry stains won't show. But I know in heaven we'll all wear white. All the girls and boys will get to bounce on the clouds, and all the fathers will have jobs and bring home pay every Friday."

Oh my! Victoria sighed. This was sad, but thank heaven for a pig who would never reveal that this little girl had to concern herself with a father's pay. She watched Alice stroke Lillian's sloping white shoulder and felt suddenly that she was eavesdropping on an intimate conversation. She should turn away, but then Alice chirped, her little voice full of excitement. "There's a huge box from France under the dining room table. It came C.O.D. all the way across the ocean on a ship, then all the way from the Port of New York on the train to the post office in Chisholm, Oklahoma. The box is full of bisque. That's china that hasn't been painted on yet. Mother's students will paint on it, but she will paint the best, biggest, most expensive things for Dr. Stevens. She's created a special pattern just for him, all gold on white china. Their family has thousands of pieces now. And Mr. Amspacher, the grocer, has quite a bit. Mother's in the china painting business."

Victoria tightened her arms around her waist and bit her lip.

"And I'm in the pig business," Alice rushed on. "When your litters have litters, this whole orchard will be solid pigs. You will be the grandmother pig, and I'll help you take care of everyone. And our family will make a lot of money. I also talked to Felicity about the two of us making pies to sell. She's already ten."

No! Victoria covered her face, then let her hands drop to her sides. The light was changing. The shadow of the house would cover Alice and her pig soon, and it would be too cold for her to stay out. She tapped on the window. Alice looked up and smiled. "Come in, sweetheart," Victoria called. "Company's coming."

~

In the kitchen Victoria scooped the sticky dough out of the bowl and plopped it on her floured board. "Oh Dan, what will Hazel Matlock think, me inviting her over to see the draperies and serving nothing but biscuits?"

"Hazel Matlock would come out here if you served nothing but gizzards. She couldn't stand to live in that town if you weren't here to keep her entertained."

"She brings me business, Dan, getting people to take lessons. And listen, she said the Episcopalians might want a Gethsemane for their vestibule. She's on the building committee."

"You'd paint Christ for a bunch of Whiskeypalians?"

"Dan, they're not all drinkers!"

"I'm teasing, Vic. That'd be grand. Don't worry about serving biscuits. The English serve biscuits every afternoon for tea. They just call them scones."

"You made that up."

"Did you see Alice out there talking to Lillian Gish?" Dan asked. "If only that pig could talk, we'd find out all Alice's secrets."

Victoria gave her dough a few light licks with the rolling pin, then smacked out a couple of dozen biscuits with her cutter. "I just dread the day we have to take Lillian to the slaughter house. Last year before she handed over the money for the pig, I explained it all to her, but you know little ones, once they get attached."

Lots of girls raised pigs, she thought as she slipped the soft disks onto the baking sheet, country girls who dreamed of state fair ribbons. But Alice's dreams were vaster—a life on the stage and money. When Alice had said she was going to put her *Prize for Expression* money into buying a pig so she could get rich, her parents should have told her to put that prize money into a decent pair of shoes. Victoria slammed the oven door. It wasn't natural for a little girl to think about making money.

"I guess you saw the box." She looked around to see if Dan nodded. "It came while you were gone into town for the paper. The thing is, I have nothing left for my students but dessert plates. And the dresser set Hazel Matlock wanted to get started on is probably in that box. The postman said he had to have his money by Monday afternoon or he'd send it back if we hadn't paid."

"That's his usual policy with you, Vic." Dan stood faced away, his hand on the hall doorframe, smoothing it as though sanding. "This is kind of a bad time. MacGaffin has been around twice already."

"I don't like that man. He comes out here talking like he's doing us a favor, saving us a trip to the bank. Bankers are not supposed to use henchmen."

"Henchmen? Vic, the way you talk. MacGaffin is Cartwright's nephew."

"MacGaffin is too rough to work in a bank, and Mr. Cartwright should keep him away from us."

"I believe, Vic, and I'm sure you also have guessed, that Mr. Cartwright hopes the visits from his unpleasant nephew will be a kind of incentive to us to pay the mortgage."

"Oh for heaven's sake, Dan, what kind of man would want to threaten a respectable family?"

"Vic, don't upset yourself. I will take care of the mortgage."

"A mortgage. It feels scandalous, shameful. This land, your family's claim, mortgaged."

He turned around sharply. "Victoria, I can't stand it when you're upset."

"I'm not really upset, I'm just trying to think ahead."

"For once, trust me. You have enough on your hands. I will figure out the mortgage situation." He turned and went into the parlor.

Little Alice stepped in from the back porch. "Alice, darlin'!" How long had she been standing there? "Come, let me fix your hair. The company's almost here." She turned Alice around and, taking hold of her braids, twisted them together into a roll along the back of the child's neck. She took a hair pin from her own head to fasten the do smartly in place, pulled a few strands from Alice's face, tucked them into the plait, then lay her hands on Alice's cold cheeks. Still such a little girl.

"I'm okay," Alice said.

"Oh, I wasn't checking for fever, Alice. I was—" She sighed. "Thanks for mopping the kitchen floor. I could never have company without you and Felicity helping out." But in her mind she was feeling not gratitude, but fear. Felicity was ten. Alice only eight. And the next one, whose existence Victoria could no longer make herself forget for long stretches during the day, would be here in late spring. She'd been old to have had a baby when Felicity was born. She pressed her hands on the small of her back and raised her bosom. Perhaps if it was a boy, Dan would take hold in a new way and find some paying work in order to be a good example to his son. The girls, he said, had her for an example and would be quite overloaded if they witnessed any more ingenuity in the house.

Most of her troubles came down to one fateful decision. Fifteen years ago, she'd been fleeing the town social when she ran into Dan Hale. Dashing toward one of the long tables to retrieve her cake stand, she saw him, leaning on one arm, his fingertips actually tapping on the base of the cake stand. The sun shone on Dan's sandy hair which feathered out from under his boater and on the fine high arch of his freckled nose. He smiled, as lean and friendly as Karl Winberg was fat and shy. Karl's mother had just made her a handsome offer she felt she needed to escape, and suddenly, here was Dan Hale appearing not to have a care in the world. She gave him a quick nod, then stooped to reach under the table for the hat box in which she had transported four dozen pale pink meringues, her contribution to the refreshments.

Dan gestured to the empty cake stand. "I've been doing a land office business here in meringue cookies. The ladies said they'd never tasted the like, and the gentlemen were stuffing them in their pockets."

She had to smile. Life to Dan Hale was all talk.

"You did this, these cattails?" he asked looking at the scene she'd painted on the top of the cake stand. She reached for the cake stand, but he framed it with his hands cupped to each side. "It quite draws you into its world, doesn't it—the water so wet, those tall leaves bent as though the breeze had just passed through. Makes you think the baby Moses might have drifted around behind those bull rushes and be there, lying in his basket, watching the sky, waiting for Pharaoh's daughter."

"Mr. Hale, goodness gracious. It's just a cake stand." No one had ever looked at her china painting like that, with such fanciful ideas.

"You don't like Biblical allusions?" he asked.

She took up the cake stand, looped the strap of the hat-box over her wrist and with a quick smile at Dan, took off across the lawn. Uninvited, he walked beside her. He'd called upon her regularly, but she'd never invited him inside the Judge's cold house. After her father was widowed the third time, he sold everything in North Carolina, including his wife's furniture and drapery, carpets and china. They'd arrived in Oklahoma Territory with nothing she could use to make a home comfortable or beautiful. Her father set up as the Justice of the Peace. She didn't know if he still had money. But she did know he was capable of violence and her efforts to clear her mind of this failed regularly.

She walked more quickly. The boys had been running foot races in front of the Mayor's house and had kicked up the dust, so she abruptly wheeled around to walk through lawns, but Dan stayed at her elbow as though they were yoked. "May I carry those?" he asked.

"No, thank you. I'm fine."

He walked almost sideways, trying to face her. "Lookie here," he said and produced from his pocket two halves of the speckled shell of a quail's egg. Her hands were full, but she inspected the subtle colors of the shells in his outstretched palm as they walked.

"Very sad about this quail," Dan said. "He was a little fella with bucked teeth and no common sense, and the girls didn't go for him."

She laughed out loud, then stared. Dan didn't have bucked teeth; he was handsome in a tender sort of way and clever, and he could be married six times over if he had any prospects. But he didn't. He had land, his family's original claim, but he and his elderly father lived out there alone like squatters—a little gardening, but no cultivated fields. What were his plans? As far as she could see, he was as opaque as this eggshell, keeping his character to himself as he drifted with no perceivable direction.

The dust from Main Street blew in their direction and she coughed. Little stones pressed into her thin shoes. Was she getting a corn? What a ghastly, old lady thing to do! Did Dan Hale realize she was older than he was? She wanted to go home and take off her shoes and huddle in the kitchen corner.

The gloom around her increased. She was walking away from an event she'd looked forward to for weeks and heading for the place that most increased her despair—a house, so dark, so devoid of warmth or comfort, it was unfit for human habitation. It was no accident she was an old maid, a girl who had trained herself to live in a shadow, to fix a bland face on loathing.

"I saw you walking with Mrs. Winberg," Dan said.

"Yes, we talked of light."

He paused before he spoke this time, and they walked more slowly. "Light is very important to a painter, I imagine," he said finally.

"Oh goodness, I'm not a painter. I just make hats."

"And that fancy cake plate? That stream with the cattails? That wasn't painting?"

The more charming he was, the more anxious she became. His easy conversation, his gentle focus upon her, were what she craved. But she stiffened her back and said, "My father says you are a man with no plans. He says the college seems to have given you a Baccalaureate in Conversation." Her own bluntness shocked her.

Dan just nodded. "Your father may be right."

The cake stand was heavy. Even the empty hatbox, dangling from her wrist, was heavy. Dan was silently matching her, stride for stride. She felt her heart crying. "Our big house is too barren inside for company. Father won't let me fix it up."

"Ah, the judge likes a spare interior."

Her father held himself above the town, calling them sod busters and cowhands, and refused to make a home in which either he or his daughter could entertain. *The judge likes a spare interior.* The stark sound of this called up her own black insides, and she mouthed the word *Mama* as she always did when she felt herself sliding into despair. ". . . so you create things for other people's houses," Dan was saying. "You're furnishing the whole town—little pieces of Victoria Jenkins's imagination sitting on dining tables and pianos and riding around on ladies' heads."

"And your mother? Is she well?" she asked trying to change the subject.

He stopped walking and leveled his gaze at her. "My mother lives in Nebraska." It was obviously a hard thing for him to say.

How could she have forgotten there was no woman out there? "I'm sorry."

"No, no. It was just that back then in the 1880's—the prairie and the wind. As a girl in Nebraska she'd been a prizewinner at anything she set her hand to, graduated top of her class at the Normal School, then became a schoolteacher. She played a little spinet at the church—the center of all her friends. But once Dad brought her here, she had no one, not for miles and miles, but me and the old man." Dan's eyes, usually glancing off any direct contact, pleaded with her for mercy.

"But you were just a boy then."

"We took her back to Nebraska." He was breathing hard, his mouth open. "Please, Victoria," he asked, "I may still seek your company?"

"Such as it is," she said. As they trudged on up the road, she marveled at the strangeness of his finding her, another lonely child.

~

After the viewing of the new draperies, to which a larger than expected crowd arrived, parking their buggies and automobiles all along the creek bank in the front, Victoria stood flushed in the hot kitchen. It hadn't been a formal party. No invitations had gone out, but she'd been huffing and puffing over that cream jersey for so many days, people were curious. The only one she recalled inviting was Hazel, just to drop in and have a look. Of course, when Mr. and Mrs. Hutchins, driving past, stopped to watch Dan through the windows putting up the rods, she told them to stop by as well. They must have told everyone else, including Mrs. Wagonard, the person Victoria least enjoyed entertaining. The woman showed up early as usual, gasping as though Victoria had imposed upon her the walk down the road and up the three front steps. Without one gracious word, she had taken hold of the doorframe, hoisted her abundance across the threshold, and headed straight for the velvet chair.

The guests had devoured six dozen biscuits with butter and peach and cherry jams and coffee and of course chocolate for the children to drink. Toward the end of the afternoon Felicity, her dark hair drawn back on her pale neck, played the piano, Chopin falling out of her fingertips as though she gave it no thought. Alice recited Mr. Stevenson's "To Alison Cunningham" that always made the mothers teary. Then everyone went home except Hazel and Mrs. Wagonard who still sat in the parlor with Dan. Hazel and Victoria had helped the guests back into their coats. Ah, to have such a woman as Hazel for a friend. She'd looked stunning when she arrived in that long velvet jacket and matching slouch tam with the one long thin feather across the front. Hazel was her best advertisement for hats.

As she gathered the cups and plates left around the living room, Victoria returned her eyes again and again to the cream draperies. Did they mean anything to the girls? Did a beautiful room reassure Felicity and Alice when there hadn't been any meat in the house for a week? When she herself was a girl, she lived in a beautiful, gracious house. And her father had had money. She had stood before his desk in the beautiful library back in North Carolina, and waited to be noticed.

After coming to Oklahoma nothing important had changed. They were stripped of possessions, and she had grown into a spinster, but she still stood before her father's desk, waiting to be noticed. He never looked up from his law books, only gestured, pen in hand. "The windows in here—" he said last week.

She hadn't replied, hoping he would give her the money to hire Old Bill to wash the windows, but he hadn't, and she hadn't enough of her mother in her to snap, Father, have you had occasion to notice you're using the Belle of the County as your hired girl! Then she remembered what she'd come for and said, "We owe for the coal." Without looking up her father had opened his drawer, taken out two paper dollars and, still staring down at his law book, held them out to her with a casual hand. With two fingers she had pulled the bills slowly from the same hand that had casually tossed aside her Mama's blood-stained pillow. This memory always flushed her with guilt.

Recalling all this, Victoria let out a little gasp, then looked at Dan, still reading the newspaper. Before returning to the kitchen, she moved the biscuits, butter and jams a little closer to Mrs. Wagonard, so the woman didn't have to squeeze her great stomach reaching.

Victoria carried the last of the dirty dishes to the kitchen where Felicity stood on a box at the sink, washing dishes while Alice dried. Hazel came out on the back porch and stood at her side as she scraped the few crumbs off the plates into the slop jar for Lillian Gish. "Is Mrs. Wagonard boarding here now?" Hazel whispered and giggled.

"Oh, mercy."

"I tell you, Vic, when I see her sitting in your parlor in that dreadful hat, without a civil word for anyone, dropping crumbs down the cushions as she Hoovers up your delicate biscuits, I want to nominate you for sainthood."

"Poor old soul. No one ever taught her any manners."

"One might look at it that way." Hazel lifted a fallen lock of Victoria's hair and taking a hairpin from her own coif, fastened it back into place. "On the other hand, one might note she has lived for nearly ten years in a gracious community and been blind to all good examples."

Victoria covered her mouth to hold back the laugh. She loved when Hazel said spiteful things, the sort of sauciness Victoria's mother had been free to let fly when they were alone. She glanced in at Felicity and Alice who seemed to be slopping along in their own world.

"And she's never going to leave," Hazel continued, "if Dan doesn't quit reading the newspaper to her like she was his old Auntie. What a swell fellow! Goodness sakes, Victoria, he may not be a Captain of Industry, but he certainly adores you."

Victoria ducked her head.

"Is that a shipment of china under the table?" Hazel asked. "Do you think the dresser set is in there?"

"I haven't had a chance to unpack it."

"I'll come next Tuesday and get started on it if that suits."

~

As Victoria worked under the lamplight, Dan read to her until his throat was so hoarse he had gone upstairs to bed. She held up the opera cape to see how much farther she had to go in attaching the fur collar. "About a mile," she whispered to herself and wondered why she'd persuaded Mrs. Woodberry to have a fox collar that reached all the way to the hem of this gorgeous flowered velvet wrap. She put one foot on the floor to push the little rocker, circled her head to ease her neck and re-crossed her feet on her mother's little embroidered footstool. She smiled recalling her mother telling of standing on this little footstool while the seamstress crept on her knees around her to pin up the hem of her wedding dress. Victoria sighed. She also had stood on the same stool to have her own wedding dress fitted, but now it was her customers who tested the creaking joints of this precious little bit of furniture while *she* was the one on her knees with the pins.

Without a warning sound, Alice appeared in the doorway like a little ghost. "Alice, what on earth? You are supposed to be in bed asleep." Victoria went on stitching, pulling her strongest needle through the pelt.

"I need to tell you something." Alice's voice was very weak and shook with the cold.

"What did you want to tell me?"

"It's an idea."

"An idea? That you have to tell me in the middle of the night?"

"There isn't much time."

Victoria stopped stitching. "What is it?"

"You need to tell Daddy to get a job, so he will get pay every Friday. That's how it works for families."

What families? Which children had she been talking to about their situation? She stared at Alice.

"This would fix all our problems, wouldn't it? Tell him that you've set your heart on it."

Victoria pulled in a long shaking breath. "No, sweetheart. I never tell him I've set my heart on anything having to do with money."

"Why not!" Alice's voice was sharp, and her face twisted with anger. "Why?"

"Alice! Hush! I'm surprised at you, using that tone of voice." Then she put her arm around Alice and spoke very softly. "Your daddy is a wonderful man, but he just will not venture out in worldly matters."

Alice nodded. Victoria knew she didn't understand and would have run upstairs having had her say, but Victoria pulled her daughter into her lap and covered the child with the delicate warmth of the opera cape.

As she rocked Alice in Grandmother Hale's little armless rocker, she felt again how much she missed Dan's mother. That dear old Quaker. When Dan had asked her about their bringing his mother to live with them, Victoria had said, "Of course. Bring her now." Dan's father had died the year before, and they were alone and in love in the house, but she had agreed to this in spite of her fear that a woman with Mrs. Hale's past might forever alter their new life together.

Victoria sighed and laid her cheek on the head of the sleeping Alice. Horrible though Olivia Jane Hale's past had been, she was like a quiet ballast in this house where things had a tendency to wobble. Her frail bones always cold, she sat in this rocker near the stove in the kitchen. After her eyes were too dim to read from her precious books of poetry, her tiny fingers darned and mended. When Felicity was born grandmother Olivia Jane could quiet that colicky baby better than Victoria herself. Victoria sniffed in a long, shaky breath. Her girls' grandmother lived here less than four years and then, just after Alice was born, she quietly died. Washing her mother-in-law's body and preparing her for the coffin, Victoria had felt an end to the pain she'd borne for so long over not being able to bring the same tenderness to her own mother.

Monday morning Alice was awake even before the gray light started between the curtains. She was tired of waiting for her sister Felicity to wake up. They needed to make a plan. Three times she'd bumped her with her bottom, but Felicity just snuggled deeper under the quilt.

One of the problems was school. She'd never missed school except when she had the dust pneumonia or her tonsils out or a few half days when she felt iffy in the stomach or Mother thought she might be a little feverish. She'd spent some of her thinking time in the dark figuring out what she'd tell anyone who stopped her on the road and asked why she wasn't in school. *I have to rehearse for a play. My school dress had to be mended. My mother needs us to take this pig to the farmer. Us* because she'd have to have Felicity, a ten-year-old, to help her. But Felicity loved school. She skipped fifth grade and was now the smartest pupil in the sixth grade. She must walk along the other side of Lillian Gish.

She gave Felicity a kick. "Mornin'."

Felicity sat up and looked around their bedroom as though she were still inside a dream. She slid off the bed and walked to the pot in the corner, pushed down her long johns, gathered her nightie into her lap and sat down. Alice, who had already used the pot two or three times through the long night, knelt on the floor in front of Felicity. "I've got a real good idea," she said.

Felicity frowned, her dark hair hanging like a tent from her middle part down over her shoulders. Alice handed her a page from the catalog, farm machinery, and clanked the lid on the pot for her. "We've got to do something this morning."

"Before school?" Felicity pulled her nightie over her head and unhooked her school dress from the back of the door. Alice did the same and started buttoning up Felicity although she herself usually got buttoned up first.

"How about you and me taking Lillian Gish to Mr. Brandt?" Alice asked Felicity's back. "I will tie a rope around her neck to lead her, but she might get afraid and run off if an automobile backfires. She needs us beside her, so she feels like we're taking a walk as usual."

Felicity whipped around. "Not sell her? You can't."

Tears stung Alice's eyes. "We need money for that box." She twisted Felicity back around and continued buttoning.

Speaking over her shoulder, Felicity said, "No, Alice, Mother wouldn't want you to do this. Lillian Gish is too young to sell. You can get a lot more for her in a couple of years."

"If Mother doesn't have china to paint–"

"Don't think about that. Lillian is your pet. Besides, we were gonna have bacon after she got big."

"I don't want bacon. The postman comes at three o'clock. Are you coming with me or not?"

"And miss school?"

"I can. No one will care."

"They'll send the truant officer."

"Don't be silly. They'll just think I have a cough. I'm doing this. I don't care what you say. It's my pig."

"You can't go by yourself."

∾ ∾

Alice kept her left hand laid gently between Lillian Gish's ears and held the rope across in her right hand. Felicity walked on the left. Alice watched the toes of her shoes walk along the road. They passed Mrs. Waggonard's house, and the dairy farm's pastures and all the long stretches of field waiting for spring.

Felicity kept looking behind them. "What if the truant officer comes?"

"Don't say that again!" Alice cried. She could already see Mr. Brandt's windmill and his silo and now the roof of his barn coming fast over the rise. Her heart pounded.

"Mother wouldn't want you to do this."

Alice didn't answer back this time. In the muddy barnyard she saw Mr. Brandt with his big bucket, dumping corn into a trough where dozens of pigs grunted and snorted and pushed against each other to get to their breakfast. Alice felt sick. She'd taken Lillian Gish her own mush this morning and tried to explain everything, but Mother had called her to come get her books, and she hadn't said it right—how happy Lillian Gish would be back with her sisters on a real farm. But now she saw the rude hogs didn't care about each other.

"Good mornin', girls. You taking the pig to school?"

"No sir," Alice said. Felicity had stopped back at the gate and just stood watching now.

"So?" Mr. Brandt said, and Alice could tell he was mad they weren't in school. She looked back for help, but Felicity was getting red in the face. "Go on then," Mr. Brandt said. "I've got another hundert hogs to feed."

"I need to sell her," Alice whispered and stepped away from her pig.

"Dat skinny shoat? Naw. You got to wait two years."

"She's very clean and nice."

"You're not old enough to sell a pig."

"You said I was a big girl when I bought her with my prize money."

Mr. Brandt pushed back his hat showing his white forehead.

"My mother needs the money."

His face screwed up, all the sunburned furrows twisting around his angry mouth. Alice was shaking. Her shoes were sinking in the muddy barnyard. She couldn't do this. Mr. Brandt's pigs were just animals. She would take Lillian home where she was happy, but her feet were stuck, and her head was stuck too and couldn't turn now to get help from Felicity.

"Your ma can't wait till it's fattened?"

"She needs the money this afternoon, please. Her heart is set on it."

Mr. Brandt looked even more angry and turned without speaking and headed back to the house.

As soon as he put the money in Alice's hand, Felicity turned and ran on down the road to school. Alice didn't try to stop her. Felicity had been crying so hard, Alice knew she was worried about disappointing her teacher. But Alice couldn't go to school yet. Her shoes were caked with smelly mud and felt terribly heavy. The wind swept up the grit from Mr. Brandt's empty field and Alice covered her nose. She'd had dust pneumonia last summer when the sand storms made the sky dark. Mother and Daddy had carried a wet sheet between them through the house, each one holding high a corner. Like a pageant, room to room, they carried the sheet, but they stayed especially long in her room, letting the sheet ripple between them to collect the dust, cleaning the air, so she could breathe.

She'd done the right thing to sell her pig, but she began to cry hard now, sobs shaking her chest and shoulders and pulling her face out of shape. The wind whipped every which way, and it took a long time for her to get back home. Mother wouldn't want her to go to school, anyway, her stomach feeling so iffy.

When she got to the house, Daddy was just opening the door to let in Mr. MacGaffin. Alice didn't like him and dashed around back to find her mother to make sure she didn't send back the box. She stopped at the corner of the house. Mother was in the side garden digging for potatoes.

~

Victoria had found only three, small potatoes, and she was surprised even to find these in this dirt she'd searched before. She sat back on her heels and looked at her dirty hands then out at the spindly rows of fruit trees she'd planted, still too young to bear. Sometimes, like now, when she was desperate for help, she thought of Hortense Winberg, a squarish woman on a cane, who had come to the ice cream social that day long ago to make her son's case to Victoria Jenkins. Swinging majestically across the wide lawn, necklaces and lorgnette chain jingling, old world black dress and huge out-of-date pocketbook swaying with her old lady gait, she approached her milliner. Her son Karl, on the edge of the lawn had shyly lifted his hat to Victoria.

"Darlink, Miss Jenkins, how is the judge's daughter?" Mrs. Winberg puffed, always full of motherly concern. "Show me vich is yours."

"Good afternoon, Mrs. Winberg. I tried meringues this time," she'd nodded to the table.

"I will go before they are all wasted on the ruffians," Mrs. Winberg said with a twinkle but did not start toward the desserts. "Your hat, as usual, is the best one. Shall I see if my Frieda likes?"

"Oh, of course." If she could sell the hat and the cake stand too, it would be a good week and this was only Sunday. She'd pay the bill at Sawyer's and order some hat frames. She smiled at Mrs. Winberg.

"Howdy," Wendell had come up behind her. His collar button was undone and he smelled a little sweaty from grinding one of the ice cream churns.

"Oh. Mrs. Winberg, have you met my brother, Wendell Jenkins?"

"Ah, I see this fine young man at church."

"How'd ya do," Wendell said and lifted his white straw. He turned to Victoria. "Vic, I saw— this morning I saw Father give—"

"He gave me a nickel to go buy him a newspaper."

Wendell tipped his hat again and left. Victoria felt the heat of humiliation in her face. Why hadn't she thought fast enough to send Wendell off on some errand, anything to postpone his pathetic begging until they were out of earshot of Mrs. Winberg? He was old enough to know better. Of course, he only wanted to have a root beer with the other boys, and she, the big sister should have had a nickel in her pocket, and now Mrs. Winberg, a good customer, knew she hadn't even that.

"Miss Jenkins," Mrs. Winberg said, seeming to have taken no notice of her embarrassment. "I have a great favor to ask."

"Of course." Ah well, even if the cake stand didn't sell, this might be a good week.

"I want you to walk with me around to Station Street."

"Now? Certainly." She offered her arm to Mrs. Winberg who took a good grip on it, and they moved swaying through the crowd out into the road.

"You have such good eyes, Miss Jenkins. Artist eyes. I want you to give me a frank opinion on a house."

There was only one house on Station Street they could be going to see. One of the oldest houses in Chisholm, it had once belonged to a doctor and had been standing empty for years. This house was so surrounded by overgrown evergreens, it had nearly vanished from sight of the street. The rumor was the price was too high, so after awhile the public had condemned the house as too dark for habitation.

To Victoria's surprise when they reached the house, Hortense Winberg pushed through the cedar bows, continued right up onto the porch and reached into her huge pocketbook to withdraw a key. As she worked the key in the old lock, she spoke as though the ideas were just coming to her. "This might make a nice house for Karl, you think?"

"It's awfully large," Victoria murmured hoping they could turn back.

"He needs his own house vonce he takes a vife. A new vife should have her own house. This is so, Miss Jenkins?"

The lock was jammed.

"Perhaps we should go," Victoria said, but Mrs. Winberg kept twisting the key. Finally the lock relented and Mrs. Winberg burst into the front hall with a great Germanic, "Ach!" The air was musty, but not as bad as might be expected. The woman leaned on her cane and held out her free hand. "Such a vide hall. You wouldn't expect." Mrs. Winberg lumbered toward the back of the house. Victoria quietly closed the door and followed.

The butler's pantry and kitchen were large but smelled like an old well, and Mrs. Winberg, squinting and sniffing about in the dark green light looked like an underwater creature, bumping here and there, counting cupboards and drawers. "The moldy drain boards, ve don't vorry. Replace mit soapstone."

Victoria followed her into the paneled dining room, trying to take as little interest as her natural curiosity would allow.

"Now the parlor. This is why you are here. Its light. Almost none." Mrs. Winberg stood in the dimness beside the beautiful carved mantelpiece, more grand than any Victoria had seen. "Up and down. Four sides of the property, those evergreens blocking. I vouldn't vont people to laugh. Hortense Winberg valls up her boy on Station Street. You have alvays been my friend. Is dark?"

"Yes, Mrs. Winberg, it's dark."

"Ah, well. So ve look upstairs, while ve're here." And with great effort, Mrs. Winberg hoisted herself, step by step, up to view the four empty bedrooms on the second floor and then on up to see the three little ones on the third.

"Ach, Miss Jenkins, let's sit," she puffed and almost fell into the window seat of a narrow front dormer. Victoria placed herself carefully upon a handy apple crate, the only loose object in the entire house. Though Mrs. Winberg made a sizable obstruction, the afternoon light streamed into the little room creating a silhouette at Victoria's feet.

"There's a lot of light up here above the trees," Victoria said, her first positive comment on the house other than her yes's and no's.

"Oh, you noticed that, too?"

How could she not notice the wonderful possibility here in contrast to a dim corner of the kitchen in which she sketched at home in the judge's house. She could paint here in any weather instead of winters painting in her coat and gloves on the back porch.

Mrs. Winberg tapped her finger against the windowpane. "Look, look, the social. We look over the mayor's house." Then abruptly she turned back to Victoria. "You know, Miss Jenkins, I married very late Mr. Winberg."

"Oh?"

"When I was twenty-five my poppa gave up on me and sent me to care for his old aunt who was dying on a farm outside Munchen. Four years I stayed on that farm caring for that old lady, seeing all my dreams go up the chimney. At last she died and before I can even go back to my poppa, a boy on the next farm said to me, 'Hortense, I'm going to America, go with me.'"

Mrs. Winberg placed a hand on each great knee, and leaned toward Victoria. "Miss Jenkins, I never would do such a thing, but when I telegrammed to my poppa that his aunt had died, he did not come. He sent back telegram saying, 'You bury her!'"

The look on Mrs. Winberg's face had changed; anger tightened the eyes and caused her jowls to shake. "He had told me this aunt vas his favorite, but now after I work four years, I discover this old lady vas nothing to him! Nothing! And I, her servant, vas less than nothing." As suddenly as it had come, the tightness left Mrs. Winberg's soft face and she said, "So I said yes to Mr. Winberg, and I haf a good life in America."

Hortense slapped her knees and leveled her gaze at her listener. Victoria felt herself sway on the apple crate. Mrs. Winberg was saying you too are old, left on the vine, as everyone knows. And there was no denying that she was now past thirty. But what was unbearable was to have it made clear that the whole town, even the immigrant baker's widow, knew in what low esteem she was held by her father.

She watched Mrs. Winberg's eyebrows slant up in the middle of her forehead like little praying hands. All Victoria had to do right now to make this dear woman happy was show a little enthusiasm for this house—just suggest that lilac bushes could hold down a property line as well as a bunch of shaggy evergreens. But she must not raise any hopes, unless, perhaps—

The glories of the house could not be denied. She should keep an open mind. And heaven knew it would be the right thing for poor Wendell whom Father squelched every day. If she married Karl Winberg, she'd always have change in her pocket for her younger brother. And Hortense Winberg would help her furnish the house. They'd do it together, making curtains, searching for second-hand pieces, and it would be so good to have this loving mother for herself. It was not the house on Station Street or being married or even the possibility at this late date that she might have children. What she craved was Hortense Winberg herself, not just to be a good customer, but to treat her as a mother would. Maybe a little bossy, very confident—*Ve don't vorry about the moldy drain boards*—a woman who cared only for her children and had money to help them.

Victoria looked away from the wild urgings of Mrs. Winberg's raised eyebrows. Why disappoint this woman whose affection she craved? But she couldn't take advantage of these good people—people who were what they seemed—as light and sweet inside as out. If she married Karl Winberg in order to gain a loving mother, she and Karl would sit downstairs in that parlor each night—Karl smiling, nodding, uttering not a word to drown out the dark howling in her head. She was not a simple person. She stood.

"Let me go down first, Mrs. Winberg. You put your hand on my shoulder."

∾ ∾

As Victoria tried to rub the dirt from the potato patch off her red, raw fingers, all the long ago images of the house on

Station Street—the walnut paneled dining room, the handsome mantle in the parlor, the sunlit upstairs room where she could paint—folded into themselves like a big picture post card, just something seen on a tour.

Just then Alice came around the corner of the house and squatted down beside her in the potato patch. Victoria was so glad to see her little girl—hair in a terrible tangle, hat hanging by its string—her teeth gritted against the sting in her nose.

"Where'd you girls go, darlin'? You didn't say goodbye."

"I sold Lillian Gish for a lot of money. It's for the china." Alice began to pull dollar bills from her coat pocket, and the wind caught one, lifting it up above the garden like a dry leaf. Alice leaped for it, but the wind drove it down again, and Victoria flattened herself on the potato mound to trap it.

"Goodness, gracious," Victoria said, sitting up and dusting off her long apron. The rest of the money fluttered, safe in Alice's grip. The wind had driven tears in clean white streaks across Alice's dusty cheeks. Victoria glanced at the house. "Let's go in, darlin', it's so cold out here." She handed the dollar back to Alice, put the potatoes in her apron pocket, and struggled to her feet. Already her swelling belly had made her clumsy.

The wind pushed them towards the house, and Victoria took hold of the railing to steady herself up the back steps. It would only torment the child to say she shouldn't have sold the pig. How could her parents have let things come to such a pass! Holding the door against the wind so Alice could enter, she suddenly knew she hadn't made a choice at all fifteen years ago. A creature like herself, a witness to wickedness, was simply ineligible for the Winbergs' easy happiness.

Inside the kitchen, Victoria sank down in a chair and opened her arms to hug Alice. Such a short little bundle.

When she opened her eyes, Dan was standing in the doorway, smiling his indelible smile. MacGaffin was behind him in the dining room, silent and waiting, as still as a dark painting.

"Hello, pumpkin," Dan said to Alice, "we were worried about you and your sister this morning. I suppose the scholarly Felicity has gone on to school?"

"I got a lot of money for my pig," Alice said.

"That's swell, Alice. It couldn't have come at a better time." Dan stepped forward and reached out his hand.

"It's for the china," Alice said softly.

"That's nice," he said.

Alice looked to her mother, but Victoria turned her head away and covered her mouth. How could MacGaffin take this little girl's money? He'd undoubtedly overheard this conversation, and if he were a decent man, he'd rush forward and say they had another week, and he'd send over a load of coal because this little girl deserved it. How could he be so heartless, leaving them here with no china to paint, no pig to fatten, all her plans cut off. She clamped her hand tighter on her mouth. And you, Dan, how can you do this, after saying you'd find the mortgage payment yourself? How can you, a grown man and a father, take your eight-year-old daughter's money rather than go out and get a job like other men. She dropped her hand.

"Dan?" she asked. "Isn't there any other way?"

He looked at her, his face naked, innocent. "Vic? Don't fuss and make things harder on Alice here." He held out his hand for the money.

"Mama?" Alice asked and Victoria had to face her and take in a shuddering breath and make a little smile and nod so that the little girl would know that it was with her mother's blessings that she would give up her plans.

Dan and Mr. MacGaffin went out the front door.

"Why did you let him do that?" Alice cried.

"Now, sweetheart," Victoria spoke softly and reached out to gather Alice in her arms. But Alice darted away and ran for the stairs. Victoria let her go. Alice deserved a good cry, and since it was all she was going to get, her mother wasn't going to try to talk her out of it.

Victoria stepped to the sink and rested her hands on the cool edge. Through the window she watched little twisters of dust dance above the empty potato patch. The pig house would be broken up and tossed into the stove. Dwindling. Everything dwindling. Victoria covered her face and sobbed, "Mama!"

THE END

RETURN TO LINCOLN
1894

And what of Dan, that sweet, broken man, that bitterly disappointing husband? What had convinced such a confident talker that he would never amount to anything?

I, Daniel Slocum Hale, would have been the runt of the litter if there'd been a litter, but I was an only child and believed I was David and Goliath all rolled into one—smart and brave, a boy who had ideas. The son of a pretty school teacher and a man who'd fought with Colonel Chamberlain in the Army of the Potomac, I thought myself a kind of eleven-year-old aristocrat with musical talent that would begin to show itself as soon as we'd settled into our new home, and Mother and I had more time for my piano lessons. Even though she was a Quaker, she was teaching me to play the Methodist hymns.

When Father galloped toward the plank-flat, purple horizon of Oklahoma Territory to register our claim, I stood on the wagon seat and waved my bandanna, hailing the start of our new life as landowners. Tomorrow morning when the claims office opened, Dad would sign his name, buying us the right to break the sod, plant, build a cabin, and make improvements on our 160 acres. After five years, an inspector would come around to judge our fences, barns and sheds, our fine house with glass windows and an iron stove, and then it would be our farm forever, and we'd buy more land with the profits.

Everything was going according to plan. In Wichita we'd stopped to buy fencing wire, meal and bacon, a bushel of sweet potatoes and enough butter to refill our crock. Right now the crock was sitting in a little eddy in the creek, and our wagon, loaded with everything worth taking from our dried up place near Broken Bow, Nebraska, stood beside the creek that ran through our claim. We had nine boxes of fruit jars with enough of Mother's pickled peaches, corn relish and canned tomatoes to go to Glory with.

As Dad rode out of sight, the sun was just bulging up, and I figured today after breakfast Mother and I'd get started making this our home. A small fire flickered where she'd made coffee and fried bread for Dad and I was sure hungry, but when she turned from her own waving goodbye to Dad to offer me a hand down from the wagon seat, her smile looked so stretched across her face, I let her take my hand and hold it after I'd jumped down.

"It's going to be a perfectly splendid day, Danny Boy. Let's walk and see every inch of our land." Her eyes were wide and sparkling. I grabbed a gunny sack and Dad's Winchester in case I saw a quail or a rabbit, and we took off, Mother walking fast and talking fast, praising the land and the sky, noting each little wild flower and calling out the names of the crops we'd plant—wheat and oats and corn, barley and sorghum and hay. And we'd have geese for feather beds and start up a library. All the way from Nebraska she'd been sober as a judge.

As we walked, I collected buffalo chips in the gunny, and when it was nearly noon, coaxed her back in the direction of the wagon. "How about some breakfast?" I said and threw down the chips near the fire.

"And the house, son, a sod cabin right now, but after the harvest, we'll have a board house with glass windows and plaster. And any can stay the night once the house is bigger, and Sister May will always have a place here, as well."

The day we left Lancaster County, Aunt May came to see us off and gave me two little books, Mr. Longfellow's poems, which she said would be improving. The other was empty, a travelogue, she said, in which I could record my own adventures. But if I ever had what you'd call an adventure—getting kidnapped by Indians or discovering gold—I wouldn't want to write it down where others could read it and tell. I'd want to do all the telling myself.

When Dad came back, Mother was quiet, all her big talk over. Dad's roan was packed with a special sod plow, more oil for the lamp and a new shovel. We dug a storm cellar, nine by twelve, and deeper, Dad said, than an ordinary dugout, his being so extra tall. This would be a cellar for storing potatoes and such, and would also serve as a shelter from tornadoes, and for the next few days, while Dad and I cut sod for the sod house, a place for us to take cover if it rained. Dad laid branches from the jacks across the top of the great rectangular hole. Then from near the creek bank, we cut big bricks of sod, overlapping them on the branches, grass side up, to make a roof. Very carefully I laid on my belly across this roof and sealed all the cracks with mud.

We used the short ladder from the back of the wagon to step down into the cellar. We made a doorframe, and Dad slanted it back to meet the roof and fastened across a sheepskin so raindrops would drain away from the opening. The ladder was too far down to be much use to me, so I just jumped onto our nice, cool packed dirt floor. It was fun to run across the plain of Oklahoma Territory and then by-golly-disappear with one leap like a prairie dog.

The earth was very dry except beside the creek, and the sod crumbled when we tried to cut more bricks to make the sod house. Dad said we needed to wait for rain. We still had the wagon sheet up and left lots of things there including Mother's best trunk with the lace curtains and her books. But everything else, including the beds, we carried down into the pitch-dark dugout. Mother didn't want to put our good carpet on the dirt floor, so we left that in the wagon rolled in the oilcloth. We didn't have room for the little armless rocking chair.

Inside the dugout Mother laid a white lace tablecloth over the biggest trunk and put her silver hairbrush and hand mirror on top, then she drove a stick into the wall and hung up their wedding picture. Mother had said she couldn't live in a dugout, so we called it the root cellar.

The first night, talking about how tired she was, she got into bed with Dad. In my little bed I lay in total blackness listening to the clods fall from the dirt ceiling onto the lid to the slop jar. Soon, I heard Dad start snoring. Then Mother got up. She took the afghan off the foot of the bed and, reaching high to grab the doorframe to steady herself, climbed up the little ladder. Since Dad's return she hadn't talked of future crops or glass windows. She hung over the wash and the cooking like an old woman. She never slept one night underground.

One night, after she'd left the dugout with her afghan, I got up and climbed out, too. The top step of the ladder barely got me head high out of the ground, but I could hoist myself out if I had to, which I did very quietly so as not to wake Dad. Like a gopher coming out of the ground, I blinked in the bright moonlight. Then I looked in the wagon, but Mother wasn't there. The oilcloth was pulled off her best trunk which stood open. I rushed to the creek. There, standing in the water in her Sunday dress, its black silk billowing out in the current, Mother stood, trying to throw a rope into a tree above. "Mother?" I called, trying to keep a steady voice and stepping further down the bank, so she could see me.

"Hello, Danny Boy." She teetered, trying to keep her footing in the stiff current. "Go on, now," she said softly, "back to bed with you."

"Yes, ma'am," I said and took a few slow steps up the bank. Then I ran, tore the hide off the dugout and screamed. "Dad, come save her."

Dad nearly knocked me down, flying out of the dugout. He ran to the creek and I raced after him.

"Olivia Jane, in God's name!" He tore into the water, knocking her down. For a moment both were under water. He came up choking and snorting, but there was not a sound from her. With her in his arms like a baby, he scrambled up the bank where he set her on her feet. He bent, still choking. She darted back to the water, but he grabbed and swung his right arm back.

"Don't," I yelled and grabbed his arm. He turned with such force, he hurled me to the ground. Then he dragged us both to the dugout. As though I was nothing, he dropped me inside. "Hand up the ladder," he yelled. I did. The hide fell across the opening. I tried to get hold of the doorframe above me, but I was way too short. Again and again, I jumped, clawing the dirt.

I stopped and dusted off my hands, then felt my way along the wall to the box with the bucket, and the cupboard and then the foot of my bed. The smell of coal oil was powerful, and I figured he'd knocked over the lamp on his scramble out. Sitting on the side of the bed in total darkness with not a sound coming through the earth, I saw her before my eyes, circled all around by the bright light on the water, her arms reaching upward. Too late I realized that this must have been the Inner Light of Christ she'd always talked about, what the Quakers wait quietly for, and there it was surrounding her like a Christmas wreath on the water. The Inner Light had come from her for some sort of Quaker baptism—something I shouldn't have spied on, something my father had wrecked. I waited a long time in the darkness for the two of them to straighten out this misunderstanding.

Trying not to breath the lamp oil fumes, I gave them plenty of time—time for her to take off her wet clothes and spread them on a bush. Time for him to build a fire, and for both of them to put on dry things. Time for them to say how sorry they were I'd had to suffer in the ground, and how they would go now and slide down the little ladder and each of them would reach down so that both could have a hand in rescuing their boy from his prison.

My bed began to make a steady squeak, and my teeth rattled before I realized too much time had passed. She was dead, and he had killed her. After another long stretch, the darkness in front of my face no longer held our fine things, the bedsteads and the quilts and the wedding picture. It was just a smothering blackness. If she *was* alive, she'd have made him let me out. He was burying her, and would saddle his roan and ride away, for he had already buried me.

~~~

I was all cried out by the time the hide was pulled away and cool air fell in.

"Son," my father's voice said, "come out now and help me." All our things came back around me—faint images in the darkness of the quilts and the wedding picture—but they looked strange and uncertain. The ladder slid down, but I pulled back into the corner.

"Come now, son. Don't be afraid."

I got off the bed and stepped up on the ladder, high enough to see my father's bare feet and his hairy shins in his shrunk up long johns. His hair was full of grass and his face was bleeding, his mustache wet, the huge, moon-lit sky behind him. I backed down the ladder, but he spoke again, his voice rough like his throat was hoarse. "Come on. It's all over." He reached in and grabbed my hand.

Dad had already tethered his roan to one side of the back of the wagon and Sally to the other. The calf nuzzled her udders. On the open tailgate between them sat a woman wearing my mother's Sunday dress. Her eyes were closed and her head hung to one side. A rope tied round and round held her arms to her sides and lashed in the folds of the black silk.

As the sky grew lighter, Dad made a thousand trips, in and out of the dugout, carrying our clothes and bedding and most of the canning. When he was finally done, he sat on the
~~~

wagon and wrote on a piece of Mother's stationary. He told me to go down into the dugout to see if there was anything I wanted and to leave the letter on the table.

It was hard to make myself go down into that dark hole. The oil lamp was cleared out, and I could hardly see. He'd left the bedsteads and most of the other furniture, but the picture was gone and all Mother's nice fix-ups. I stood in the light from the door and read the letter:

To any man who reads this

You are welcome to take shelter on my claim. The water in the crek is good, and hard tack is in red box under the big bed. My family has been called away on account of sickness. We will return by erly October.

James Elliott Hale
August 31, 1894

After he pulled me out of the dugout, Dad handed me up to sit on the wagon seat beside him, and here I was in Mother's place. We rolled away from the creek onto the bald prairie where there'd be no place to hide if Mother and I made a run for it. The wind pushed us from the west, tearing at the wagon sheet, rattling all the hanging pots and pans like bones clattering. I had no choice about going, but where he was taking us, I didn't know. I knew only I mustn't get separated from her again.

"Where're we going?" I asked

"Back to Nebraska."

"She looks crooked. Why'd you tie her up?"

My father wiped his hand down his mustache and looked long to the north. "Your mother's got a cryin' sickness. We gotta keep her safe."

The rest of the day my mind kept grinding, over and over, why hadn't I managed to pile up some furniture and climb out to save her from the licking he'd given her? What kind of boy was I?

❧ ☙

When Dad untied her the first night, so she could change her clothes, she moved about like a china doll that would break if she bumped anything. While he made the fire, I walked around to where she had sat back down on the tailgate. Something about her, just sitting there, not working, made me timid. Her hair was half loose, a bluish bruise showed on her chin, and her blouse was buttoned up crooked. "Mother?"

"Your mother's not worth much this evening," she said and I could tell it cost her a lot just to get the words out. I wanted her to say something more, but seeing the bruise and that extra little button with no buttonhole there at her throat made me back away.

❧ ☙

I'd hardly ever studied my own dad's face, but as we rode along side by side on the wagon seat, I watched him out of the corner of my eye. It was a long, tanned, thin-lipped face, and his teeth weren't very pretty. Every now and then he'd screw up one side of his mouth like a tooth was twinging him. It gave him a conniving look. He shaved his chin every morning, but lately had forgot about trimming his mustache. This was something Mother usually did for him late at night after she was in her nightgown, and I was supposed to be asleep, but I saw them once. Being more than a head taller than her, he had sat on a chair with his knees spread so she could stand right in front of him. He had his hands around her waist, big fingertips stacked up along her backbone. She held a comb in one hand and her sewing scissors in the other.

"He's gotten to look such a murderous soldier," she said to him, "I must trim his mustache." To my amazement, even though she held the blade of her scissors right against his upper lip, he began to sway her waist back and forth a bit.

"Mind now," she said softly. I ran back and jumped in bed.

Now, not only was his mustache looking all scraggly, but he leaned his great self forward, elbows on his knees as he drove the team, like an ordinary sod buster instead of a brave soldier. I realized I'd puffed up a great idol out of very ordinary materials, and what he really was, I did not know.

After a few days Mother couldn't even sit up to ride and lay on the feather bed in the wagon box behind Dad and me. She'd cry softly for miles, and when I didn't hear her crying, I heard her grinding her teeth, trying not to cry. At night I slept alone in the wagon, and Dad slept on the ground with his arm around her.

He avoided settlements, making wide circles around them. One afternoon, we camped in some trees in sight of a little town. After we'd staked the team and Sally, Dad started to saddle up his horse. "Are you gonna bring a doctor?" I asked.

"No," he said, "supplies." He brought the milking stool out of the wagon, sat Mother on it, tied her hands behind her back and tethered her to the wagon tongue. He left me the Winchester. "Don't untie her," he said and swung his leg up over the roan.

For a long time I stood guard on my own mother, wanting to untie her, but somehow afraid to. Suddenly, I had a great idea. Inside the wagon I rummaged in Mother's best trunk and found the rolled up paper keyboard. Before we left Nebraska, she'd glued together many sheets of paper end to end until she had a strip long enough. Then with her ruler, she drew all the black and white keys so it looked like the keyboard on the piano at church. We called it our spinet.

Almost every evening after dinner on the trip south to Oklahoma Territory, she would roll our spinet open on the tailgate and lay a plate on both the bass and treble ends to hold it flat. I would bring the folded blanket from the wagon seat to make myself higher on the nail keg for she was very particular always about my elbows and my fingers being in just the right position to strike the keys. "Do," she would sing when I touched my thumb to the paper keyboard. "Re," she would sing when I touched D. She would watch my fingers carefully, so she didn't sing what the note was supposed to be, but the key I actually struck, and if it was the wrong key, she would sing out like a crow on the terrible wrong note no matter how lightly I touched it. I hated hearing my mother ever make an ugly sound, so I strived always to play perfectly.

Standing in front of her, I held out our spinet where she could see it. Her head rested against the wagon wheel, but she looked sidelong at me. I sat down on the ground and unrolled the keyboard, weighting each end with little stones so it would lie flat.

"Look, Mother." I put my thumb on middle C. "Do, re, mi, fa, sol."

She was silent except for her breathing.

"Let's do 'Truehearted, Wholehearted,'" I said. This was a marching kind of hymn, a good boys' hymn, Mother used to say, because you could sing it plain and loud. I put my right hand on the keyboard, fourth finger on the F to start. I sang and thumped it out.

> *True-heart-ed, whole-heart-ed, faith-ful and loy-al,*
> *King of our lives, by thy grace we will be;*
> *Un-der the stan-dard ex-alt-ed and roy-al,*
> *Strong in thy strength we will bat-tle for thee.*

I hadn't sung in so long, and cracky though my voice was, my singing gave me heart, and I pushed on for the refrain:

> *Peal out the watch-word! Si-lence it nev-er!*
> *Song of our spir-its, re-joic-ing and free;*
> *Peal out the watch-word! Loy-al for-ev-er!*
> *King of our lives, By thy grace we will be. A-men.*

I let my Amen ring up to heaven the way she'd taught me and felt I'd done us both some good. But when I turned to see if she was as swelled up as me, she was staring glassy-eyed at the ground, her face wet. I lifted the stones and let the paper keyboard roll itself back up.

Nothing ever raised her spirits better than the spinet, so I knew she was too sick for anything I could do, and the idea of the two of us singing together was foolishness.

∾ ∾

One night we were camped on a rise above a creek and could see Wichita, Kansas, in the distance. I unhitched the team and staked them to graze while Dad went off to hunt. Mother had hardly moved all day, and Dad didn't tie her up, just lifted her from the wagon and set her on the three-legged milking stool. After gathering some firewood, I went to the back of the wagon to untie Sally so's to move her and the calf to some good grass. When I came around the wagon, I saw Mother running down the hill toward the creek. I dashed after her, but Dad, coming along the bank, had seen her too, and I watched him grab her arm and swing his fist. She dropped straight down without a sound, and he caught her and carried her back up the rise.

He stooped to set her back on the milking stool. Putting his arm under her neck, he ladled water over her head and rubbed it on her face, his hand dark against her white cheeks. She opened her eyes half way, but wouldn't look at him.

"Light the fire, then go back down near the water and bring up those jack rabbits," was all he said to me.

As I came back up with the rabbits, two huge ones, a man came through the trees leading his horse. He was not so tall as Dad, and his coal black hair and long, thin mustache made me take him for a pirate. But I was so glad to see another person, I wanted to take hold of that pirate's arm and make him sit down.

Seeing the man, Dad gathered a big breath and rose from Mother's side. The man glanced at mother, looking broken there against the wagon wheel.

"I see you got troubles," he said. "I'll move on."

I took hold Dad's sleeve. He said, "Have something to eat before you go."

"Much obliged." The man squatted down beside our fire, and Dad started skinning the rabbits. Up close, the man looked nothing like a pirate, cause his eyes were blue. He said his name was O'Riley, and I figured after Dad was asleep, I'd tell O'Riley about Dad holding Mother prisoner. O'Riley and I would take Mother into Wichita to a fine doctor who would give her a tonic for her crying sickness. Maybe she and I would stay on there awhile till she felt strong enough to go back to the claim.

"I've got a job in Wichita," O'Riley said. "Did ya see the electric lights?"

"Uh huh," Dad said.

"Got a job in the stock yard. Biggest outfit I ever saw." This man was a talker, and I guessed he could tell Dad wasn't. I walked through the trees and looked off to the North, and there was Wichita, with little glowing electric lights here and there, the grandest sight.

Dad fried bacon and then the rabbits and some potatoes too and opened a jar of Mother's corn relish. I coaxed Mother to eat some of the potatoes, but she wouldn't touch anything else and went to lie down in the wagon. The men ate big heaps of food, and Mr. O'Riley talked while he chewed, telling one story after another about being a cowboy and before that fighting Indians and before that being in the Union Cavalry. I was surprised Dad didn't say anything about serving with Colonel Joshua Chamberlain in the Army of the Potomac, but he did allow as how he'd grown up in Maine and moved on to Nebraska in '69, and it made me think about how old he was. I wanted him to tell O'Riley about the battles he'd fought in and about how he'd given the Colonel his water at Gettysburg.

But I didn't say a word, not wanting anything to stop O'Riley's talking. I lay on the oilcloth next to where Dad was sitting on his saddle raking the coals. As O'Riley started another story about licking the Rebels, I pretended to go to sleep, so they'd take no notice of me.

Dad stirred a little when O'Riley said he'd been there when the Union troops freed the men from the Andersonville Prison. "Never, if I live to be a hundred will I ever see anything more murderously horrifying than the sight of those poor boys."

Dad put his hand over my ear, but I could still hear O'Riley talking about men's ribs and black tongues. I felt Dad take in a breath. "My twin died at Andersonville," he said.

"Aw, Jesus!" O'Riley said, "And me going on about the place. I sure am sorry for your brother. A mighty hard thing to get past."

"Had to swallow it down." Dad's stick stirred the coals.

"You, yourself?" O'Riley asked.

"Colonel Chamberlain."

"Ah, the finest gentleman and a valiant soldier. Very learned and judicious, they say. To have served under such a man, you are fortunate indeed. And after the war, you—?"

The business about my dad's twin brother, I'd got from Aunt May, so that was no surprise. She'd said the Andersonville prison was a terrible place to die, and that had puzzled me because if you're dying anyway, what difference does it make where you are? It did give me some satisfaction that Dad had finally mentioned Colonel Chamberlain, and I wanted to hear more, but sometimes when I'm pretending to be asleep, I am asleep. Next thing I knew, they were talking about something completely different.

"—rough and fine, both of us old for marriage," Dad was saying, "but she was the most peace a man could ask for. That's all I was looking for after the war." It didn't sound like Dad, going on like that, and I think he must have surprised himself, because he was quiet for awhile, and the next thing I remember hearing was O'Riley saying, "That's what you oughta do, the Santa Fe, right over there in Wichita. Take her on the train. You can be there in two days. The way your goin', the cow and the calf and all."

Dad didn't answer.

"Leave the little tow head in Wichita. Any good boarding house'll keep an eye on him 'till you get back. I'd do it myself, but—"

ᔕ ᔓ

We didn't take the road into Wichita, but skirted around to the West. The wind had come up again and rocked us, making the going slow. I could see the railroad and the stockyard in Wichita and knew Mr. Riley was already there working. Dad had sold him the calf, so if it hadn't been for the wind, we might have rolled along a little faster, arcing back to the north. We were headed back to Broken Bow. It made sense, taking Mother back, so Aunt May could nurse her. The only problem was when Aunt May saw the rope burns on Mother's wrists and found out he'd hit her and it looked like he'd starved her besides, she'd skin Dad alive. Quakers weren't violent. They wouldn't hit you with a stick, but Aunt May would call down the wrath of God on anyone who'd lay a hand on her dear little sister. It was hard to believe he'd let himself in for that. He'd always been standoffish where Aunt May was concerned.

Late the next morning, after we'd been on the trail awhile, I asked Dad, "When your twin brother was in that prison, where were you?"

He whipped around at me, his brown teeth clinched and shouted, "You mean why didn't I just take a company of men and ride into Georgia and make 'em let all those poor boys go? Is that what you're asking? Eh!"

My mouth was too dry to speak. He'd never shouted at me like that, and I had to swallow hard to keep from crying.

ᔕ ᔓ

Mother did not rest well on the ground. From the look of him during the day, Dad wasn't getting any sleep either. After many nights of this, he told me to sleep on the ground, so she could have the wagon box. He made a little cuff from an old bridle and at night fastened her ankle to a light chain he held the end of out on the ground where he and I slept, his head on his saddle, mine on the bolster.

The chain raked against the edge of the wagon in the night and made me think of the slaves so long ago my father had fought to free. Shame stung my eyes. My mother was nothing more than a tethered beast, and I was doing nothing to rescue her.

Sometimes when we'd pass another wagon, Mother would cry out, "Help! Help me!" Folks would stare at us, and I'd try to flash them a pleading look. Not too long after she started doing this, we were looking for a campsite near a lake in the middle of Kansas, and a man on horseback caught up with us and called out for Dad to halt.

Dad pulled up the team, and the man, on a tall, black horse rode up beside us so he and Dad were eye to eye.

"My name's Lester Starr. I'm the Sheriff of Marion County."

"James Hale."

They didn't shake hands. The sheriff tipped up the brim of his hat. "Some folks back in Aulne said they heard a distressful sort of cry. Just could I take a look in your wagon?" I gripped the edge of the seat board. Help had finally come.

Dad scratched the back of his neck and squinted past me, far into the east, hatching up a plan of escape, I figured. He turned back to the sheriff. "Sir," was all he said, and he handed me the reins and climbed down, not even reaching for the Winchester that was right under us. Broad-chested, thick-fisted and much younger than Dad, the sheriff would win for sure if they got into a fight.

The sheriff got off his horse and after a tiny nod from Dad followed him over to some bushes out of earshot. Still as a post, just the tail of his coat lifting in the breeze, Dad did no more talking with his body than he did with his mouth, so it looked like the sheriff was the one pleading innocent. Pretty soon the sheriff swung out a thick paw, shook hands with Dad, mounted his horse, and rode away. I was a yellow-bellied coward.

That night two women came to our wagon. One was the sheriff's mother, Mrs. Starr, and the other was his wife. They brought a dishpan, a towel, and a bar of soap that smelled like lavender. They set Mother's biggest pot to boil on the fire, then, carrying a lantern, they both climbed into the back of the wagon.

I went and sat quietly in the dark off to the side of the wagon. Because of the lantern, the wagon sheet glowed like a moon. Through it the rockers on the chair looked like dark horns hanging above the heads of the two women. The young one knelt at Mother's feet and held the pan while the old lady undid Mother's clothes. At first I thought I heard a man's voice answer the women, but it turned out to be mother's voice, broken by all her crying. I moved closer.

"May I just lift you head, Mrs. Hale?" the old lady said. I could see their shadows and could hear the water as the old lady wrung out the cloth.

"You are in no pain, Ma'am?" the younger one asked.

"No pain in my body."

"Then it is a sickness of the soul?" the young one asked.

"Leave her be, Hazel," the old lady said. "Now the other arm, Mrs. Hale." The old lady was as gentle as if she'd been washing a baby.

"But if it is a matter of the soul, then surely we should send for Reverend Rawlins," the one called Hazel said.

"Leave her be. It is the melancholy. Now Mrs. Hale, I'm just going to send Hazel for a fresh pan of water, so I can wash your hair if you'd like."

The younger woman climbed out and rushed to the pot on the fire to fill the pan.

"I think I've got all the pins now. Such beautiful chestnut hair, Mrs. Hale. Don't mind Hazel, she is young and quite taken with the new preacher in town." Like a woman carding wool, Mrs. Starr drew the hairbrush through my mother's long hair.

Hazel rushed back with the pan, but before she could climb into the wagon, a bundle of my mother's clothes was thrust out in exchange for the pan of fresh water. Hazel took the clothes back to the pot and began to stir them into the water. There was no sound from the wagon except the dripping of water as Mrs. Starr held my mother's head above the pan and ladled the water over it.

Hazel made short work of the wash, ran down to the lake to rinse, then laid my mother's dress and petticoats across a branch to dry. She rushed back. "Isn't this just the kind of case Reverend Rawlins was describing, the total absence of hope?" Hazel said, climbing back in.

"Is there something clean I can help you put on, Mrs. Hale?" Mrs. Starr asked softly.

"But it's always the person's fault if there is no hope; it's a sure sign the Devil had gotten in. And he got into her life because she harbored doubts. That's what makes way for the Devil. A Doubting Thomas is what she is, and you can see the results."

"Ah, that's better," Mrs. Starr sighed. "There's nothing like clean clothes and clean hair, is there, Mrs. Hale."

"You're only pleasuring the body," Hazel wailed, "when we should be driving out the Devil."

Suddenly, Dad was standing not ten feet behind me. "Thank you for coming and doing for Olivia Jane," he said in a booming voice as he walked to the wagon.

Hazel's head poked out. "My preacher can drive out this devil. He knows the truth."

"Thank you for coming, ma'am."

The women finished up quick after that and left. I felt very uneasy. "But Dad, if that preacher could help her."

"Your mother has always said, 'Men's minds are small compared to God's, and those who claim to know God completely have the smallest minds.'"

That was the sort of thing that was beyond me. I climbed up in the wagon and sat beside Mother. She smelled of lavender and the woman had left the soap.

"It was to be a wedding present for her niece," Mother said in her croaky voice. "Mrs. Starr left it for me."

"That was nice of her. Did you get presents when you were married?"

"Oh, my, yes," she said, and the tears started down her cheeks, but she was smiling. "My friends embroidered napkins and table cloths, and one crocheted about a mile of lace meant to go on the edge of a sheet and a pair of pillow slips. I never did anything with it. Sometimes I think about giving it to your bride."

"I don't have a bride."

"Not now, of course. You're just a boy, but you will grow into a wonderful man and have a loving wife."

"I will?"

It seemed beyond belief that I would grow into a man, but the idea of a loving wife was worth a lot, a girl I would never hit, who'd make lace and sing and fix up our place. I swallowed hard.

~ ~

Finally, we got shut of Kansas. We'd been heading north for a couple of hours since breaking camp and there was a steady breeze. Mother lay sleeping in the wagon box, her little bones nothing more than an armload of sticks. I wanted to run away with her before she starved to death, but I didn't know if he'd kill me.

"Dad?"

"Yeah."

"Sometimes, we're rolling along here, and I wonder what your thoughts are."

He slowly turned his head to frown at me, then wrenched the side of his mouth with the bad tooth—an uglier face I'd never seen. "You mean my thoughts right now?"

"It's just I feel suspenseful all the time."

He shook his head. "I'm thinking that harness is wearing through," he said gesturing between the horses.

How lucky he was to have a brain like that—one that stayed fixed on such things while my boy's brain was tormented worrying the rope was cutting her wrists, and feeling a sickening shame about the chain. Would she ever forgive us? But I felt even worse now knowing that what was happening to me—my heart being gnawed at by a sharp-toothed weasel—was not happening to Dad. We were two different kinds.

His mind was still, and his voice calm whether talking to me or to Mother or to some stranger he was asking for water. It must have been the soldiering that had made him so calm.

Maybe this was his Courage which I'd imagined him wearing into battle like a knight's suit of armor. He had Courage and now he was inside it, calm and easy, feeling no hungry weasel, nor lying awake at night gritting his teeth not to cry.

∾ ∾

One evening in order to rest my mind, I took the paper keyboard out of Mother's trunk, carried it away from the wagon and weighted the ends with stones. I felt shy about putting my fingers to the keys without Mother there to sing, but as soon as my thumb touched the middle C, her voice, as clear as could be, sang beside me. Her body wasn't there, but somehow in my fingers, like I was playing on a real instrument, was the power to bring her voice. After that I kept the rolled up paper piano in my own satchel with my Longfellow book and my empty travelogue.

We'd been sticking close to the banks of the Big Blue for three days, and it had brought us way into Nebraska, almost to Beatrice where we camped. They must have had a little rain in the area, because the air was sweet in the morning. Dad had made Mother swallow a little mush before he laid her back in the wagon. I'd just come up from washing the mush pot and the bowls and saw him looking at the pink dawn light on the river.

"From Beatrice there's a good road straight north to Lincoln." He said this, then picked up his saddle, always the last thing he loaded, but he stood still, didn't turn toward the wagon.

"Aren't we heading east to Broken Bow?"

"No."

"We're not taking her to Aunt May?"

"No."

"Why would we want to go to a big old place like Lincoln?"

"There's nothing left of our place in Broken Bow. All blown away."

I realized then we were whispering. "But Aunt May's there, teaching school."

"If the school's still there." He didn't move, just held the saddle and stared at me. The morning breeze shook the hickories with a fluttery pink light that made my Dad come and go before my eyes. "We're taking your mother to the state insane asylum in Lincoln. We'll be there by evening tomorrow."

He left me under the trees with the mush pot and plates dripping against my shirt. I'd heard of the asylum. That's what the kids in the schoolyard meant when they said, "They should send you to Lincoln." It meant you were crazy and should be locked up in the mad house. Bad as I thought he was, I'd never guessed this was what he was up to, locking her up with strangers.

I managed to put the pot and the bowls away in the slotted box before I climbed aboard, but I don't recall much until I lay down beside my mother that evening. Dad was staking the horses beside a creek.

"Mother?"

"I'm sorry, Danny," she said.

"Do you know where we're going?" I asked.

She nodded and the motion squeezed tears out of her eyes.

"Are you afraid?"

"I told him, before I ever went into our creek, to take me back to Lincoln, but he said I'd always got better before, and I should hang on. But now, I know I cannot bear it there. I have not the strength."

"You've been there before?"

"After each of your sisters—"

"Yes?"

"After each birth a sort of black grief—Just minutes old, the poor little things, too weak to suck and then—" She held out her empty hands.

"Aunt May told me."

"I cried for weeks. The preacher at the asylum said I needed to accept God's will and let the grieving go. And I did get better, each time, and came home. But Danny, even when you were born and lived, I was filled with a despair that was in every way the opposite of what I should have felt with a fine baby son, so bright and with such a vigorous voice." She paused and smiled as she always did about my loud bawling. Then she clutched my hand. "Inside me, like a flood of black ink through all my blood and thoughts, a kind of hopelessness I just can't shake off."

"And you feel that way now?"

She nodded, and I saw some gray at the edge of her dark hair and wrinkles around her hazel eyes. She took a deep shuddery breath. "I don't want to be a burden to you and him. I figure a mother who can't work should be put away, but tonight—" She choked. "Please, Danny Boy, let me go so I can end this pain. I know what to do this time."

"I'll help you," I said. "I'll tell him I'm going to read to you after supper."

Dad nodded and seemed glad when I told him about reading to mother. I started with her favorite Psalms, reading clearly and with meaning as I'd been taught. I heard Dad settling down by the fire and realized he might be listening, too. So after I'd read from the letters to the Corinthians and the Ephesians, I turned back to Genesis, not the exciting part about making the world, but the begats. I read slowly in a sleepy voice: "And Arphaxad lived five and thirty years, and begat Salah. And Salah lived thirty years and begat Eber." I let longer and longer pauses between the words and read softer and softer. Mother's eye were bright and darted from my face to stare through the wagon sheet in Dad's direction. I was more awake than I'd ever been, but sure enough, Dad began to snore—louder than usual, deeper asleep, I guessed, than he'd been on the whole trip.

Lying on my back, I crooked up my knees and pushed myself along, worm-like till I could reach under the seat for the Winchester. Mother's head was raised, but I gave her a sign not to move until I had wormed my way back to the tail-gate, holding up the rifle and repeating over and over, "And Arphaxad lived after he begat Salah four hundred and three years and begat sons and daughters."

I helped Mother down, and we moved quietly out of the moonlight into some willows along the creek bank. At first we ran just to put some distance between us and the camp, then I took her hand and tried to lead her around, so we'd get back on the road in the direction to head back to Beatrice. But she kept pulling in the direction of the water. "We must get to the road or we'll get lost in the dark," I whispered.

"You go," she said. "Leave me here by the still water."

"Not now," I gasped, but before I could turn her, I heard a crashing behind us.

"Oh Danny, don't let him take me!"

I raised the gun, aimed and fired twice. My father cried out and fell in the underbrush. Then there was a terrible silence. I didn't breathe. My mother stood beside me like a stone. Finally a voice came. "Olivia!"

She ran to him. It was dark all around.

My father rolled onto his back. Mother opened his shirt and slid her hand in to feel about on his chest for wounds. I stooped beside her.

"Help me get him to the wagon."

All the way to the wagon Mother talked very sharply to him. "Come on, James, you're not so bad off you can't get you legs under you." And the same to me. "Get the smallest pot and bring water to a fierce boil. Now!"

He crawled into the wagon, and she made him lie on his side.

"One bullet has gone in but not come out," she said as she felt along his back.

The worst part was waiting for the water to boil. I held a clean cloth pressed against his side to hold in the blood while she sharpened her little pocket knife, round and round on the flint as she muttered, "Yea though I walk through the valley of the shadow of death," over and over she prayed; round and round she drove her knife against the flint until I feared there would be no blade left. I held the lantern while she made a slit in my father's flesh and pried out the bullet from between two back ribs. He passed out while she was operating.

∾ ∾

We camped there for ten days, and the whole time Mother was near her old self. She made Dad lie completely still so his blood wouldn't start again. I hunted for meat to make him strong. She skinned or ripped the feathers off anything I brought her and cooked the things Dad and I had missed—dumplings and fritters. She washed all the blood from our clothes and bathed Dad's head with a damp cloth off and on all day and all night, and once his fever was gone, she repacked all our gear and swept the ground around the fire.

When not out hunting, I stayed at her side and tried not to be useless while I waited for her to speak. I might have killed my father—a thought too horrible to let my mind rest on. But the big question for me was whether I had been a bad son to my mother as well, and I waited for her to tell me.

"Will you let him get up tomorrow?" I asked as she and I sat beside the fire.

"Yes, tomorrow. His color is good, finally. A day longer, and he'll be too weak to stand."

"What will we do then? There is no reason to—"

"Your father will decide."

"But you are all yourself again. Working."

"I work to stay ahead—" She was sitting on a log, not in the pretty, lady way she once did with her back straight and her feet tucked in together. She sat now bent over, her knees spreading her skirt like a farmer's wife.

"Ahead of what, Mother?"

Her eyes slowly raised from the embers, but they were not my mother's eyes. For the first time since the shooting, she began to cry.

"I'm sorry, Mother, I didn't mean—"

She jumped up and grabbed the broom and began to sweep. "Though the waters roar and foam though the mountains tremble," she muttered as fast as she swept, and I realized I had been a bad son to her all along.

∾ ∾

A wind from the north had driven straight into the wagon all day, slowing us, telling us not to keep on in this direction, so it was late when we came upon the awful towers and barred windows of the State Asylum in Lincoln. The moon, coming and going from behind blowing clouds, would light up the place one minute, then spare us the next. All day I'd sensed Mother growing stiller inside herself like a room in which the candles were being snuffed out one by one. A Quaker with no more inner light, she lay in the wagon as though already in a coffin and neither cried nor muttered any Bible verses.

Dad went inside himself as well, growing even duller than he was already. But I didn't hate him. I envied him. He was going inside his Courage, and he would be safe and calm there. As for me, I felt I was going to a hanging—one where I, myself, would have to hold the rope.

The place looked like a terrible castle with turrets and an iron fence all around. I listened for cries from the prisoners, but couldn't hear because Dad didn't drive the team up to the door, but stopped outside a big iron gate. He handed me the reins. Lifting the latch on the gate, he walked with great swift strides across the yard, his coattail flapping in the wind. The moonlight was steady now casting a long, skinny shadow out from my father's feet on the short, dry grass, bleaching it to look like snow. I'd not seen snow nor packed a snowball in a hundred years.

Dad banged a great iron ring against the door, and the sound struck my chest and started me breathing again. The door opened and he slipped in. Mother lay so still, the thought crossed my mind she might be dead—what she'd wanted all along though I'd been too stupid to see it.

After a while, Dad came out with two thick looking men, one carrying a lantern. I watched the three coming across the yard. I had but to slap the reins to haul me and Mother away from this place, but I knew there was nothing the likes of me could do to save her.

"Olivia Jane," Dad whispered and opened down the tailgate. "I cannot carry you in, so you must walk. There are two men out here, but I've told them not to lay hand on you."

Mother said nothing. I made myself turn and look. By the light of the lantern I watched my father gather the skirt hem about her ankles and pull her from the wagon with no more protest nor cooperation than he'd get from a bolt of canvas. He set her on her feet. Then he climbed in and reached up to unhook Mother's little armless rocker and set it on the ground. While she waited, he slid out her trunk with all our finest things and our best rug. He nodded to the men and took hold of her hand. They all started toward the building, the man with the lantern going ahead, carrying the trunk on one shoulder, and the other with the rocker and the carpet, walking behind. Before they got to the door Mother let go Dad's hand and folded her hands on her waist.

The man with the lantern kicked open the door, so Mother never paused, but walked right across the threshold followed by the man with her rocker and carpet. The door closed. Dad stood alone in the yard.

"Mother!" I ran across the yard. "Stop her, Dad!" I ran past him and banged my fists on the door. "We can't leave her here alone." He grabbed my wrists, but I twisted away and kicked him. "Get her out, Dad. Get her out. She's ours, Dad. Get her out!"

He grabbed me up and ran and didn't stop until we were outside the gate. "I hate you. I hate you." I screamed and kicked. But his iron arms stopped my breath. He held me against him and laid his hand on my head to press my cheek against his wet neck. "Swallow it, Danny," he whispered. "Swallow it down."

⁂

That night Dad and I started back to our claim in Oklahoma Territory. I lay in the wagon box a lot the first few days of the trip. I felt he hadn't loved her and therefore it was not a sin what he'd done. I had loved her, but not enough. She wouldn't have got that crying sickness if I'd loved her more.

Now and then, I raised my spirits by playing the paper piano in the back of the wagon. Mother's voice was growing fainter, so I had to sing the notes myself, but that did no good, for I always sang the right note no matter where my dumb fingers struck. It was a kind of cheating.

One afternoon as I rolled up the paper, I stared at my father's back, the knobs of his spine arcing forward, elbows resting on his knees. He was so bent the underside of his hat brim was all I could see of his head. I climbed forward to sit beside him.

"Are you lonely, Dad?" The cheek jerked with the bad tooth, but he kept looking ahead to the southwest. Finally, he nodded—one dip of his scraggly face.

"Then I'll stay up here," I said. I knew I would need to do all the talking, but that was fine with me because whenever I stopped talking, I could feel the weasel sneaking up on me. The names Andersonville and Lincoln Asylum kept coming into my mind, and I knew I'd feel better if I was sitting next to a soldier.

THE END

THE LUCKIEST LITTLE THING IN THE WORLD
1887

Some wives run away. Victoria's own mother escaped as a ghost.

A photograph was taken of my parents on their wedding day in Asheville, North Carolina, November 1870. I came upon this cardboard-framed portrait wrapped in a remnant of gray silk in their bedroom highboy. Ten or eleven-years-old at the time, I worked with trembling fingers to unwrap something Mama clearly wanted wrapped up. But I knew it immediately for what it was, and I couldn't breathe. The groom in a beautiful frock coat looked perfectly frozen, standing straight, chest out, his mustaches curled up, his tall hat reverently balanced on his palm. The girl in a silk bonnet seated to his left appeared, by the fierce look in her eyes, to be trying to stay still. But what had been easy for the groom had been beyond her. And the mouth was blurred as though she had started to say something.

"Oh, Victoria, darlin', kindly put that back as you found it," Mama said. I hadn't heard her come up behind me, and I jumped. "That ruined thing," she said. "See how my mouth is all catty-wampus. A regular mess. Put it away. Please."

I looked down at the photograph. It didn't look ruined to me. She had many times told me how Father, a lawyer, a man of property, had fallen in love and rescued her from want and desolation. He married her when she was just sixteen. I thought of Mama in the flames of the war and in the mean times that followed, and my heart raced. She must have believed herself to be the luckiest little thing in the world to ascend from the ashes of a small farm near the Smoky Mountains into the shelter of society in Asheville, North Carolina. Society in all the cities of the South was in grave distress in those days because of the loss of homes and property and businesses, but there were men like my father, Gilbert Alphonse Jenkins, who made a quick recovery. The idea of the orphan girl on her wedding day was terrifying and romantic. And here in my hands was a proof of the stories Mama had told me of their love.

Ever after that first discovery, I would often unwrap the dry silk to gaze at the picture which seemed more and more important to me as the regular patterns of my life dissolved. Last spring Mama removed herself from that bedroom to a smaller room down the hall.

At dinner my little brother, Wendell, only five, had asked, "Mama, why did you sleep in the little room?"

Father scowled and Wendell lifted his hand to shade his eyes as though Father's face were a fierce sun. Father reached out to pull his hand down. This caused Mama to sing out brightly, "Wendell, darlin', I have removed myself to the sewing room until I'm cured of this pesky cough. Victoria, dear, tell your Father about your paintings."

"That St. Pierre woman wasn't here again today, was she?" Father asked.

"They are going to hang them up on Contest Night all over the school house. Just think, our daughter so accomplished at fifteen."

"She's nothing but a gossip," Father pushed on. "Bessie said she was here today."

"Well," Mama said, extravagant and playful, "if Bessie said she was here, she must have been here. Isn't that right, Victoria? I myself did not see her, but Mrs. St. Pierre would never speak ill of *you*, Gilbert," Mama said, her eyes twinkling. "She is one of your admirers."

Mrs. St. Pierre, a woman of strong opinions and coarse manners, forced a visit upon us often. In her garish mismatch of second-hand laces and furs, she reeked of perfume and unaired trunks. I had ceased taking her upstairs to visit Mama where she invariably clucked about, shifting the covers and recommending brutal remedies such as the blistering. I took upon myself the burden of entertaining this unrefined woman.

∾ ∾

Bessie was our Irish hired girl who, though she rarely went anywhere except out to do the shopping, seemed to know a great deal about what went on in Asheville as well as the whole of the Buncombe County. Bessie, her red face always moist, her carrot hair always frizzing down in her eyes, was the one to tell me of anything exciting—calves born with two heads, girls sent away by their families, or murders—"She shot 'im dead with his own rifle, cartridges in plain sight on the Chinese carpet." Bessie was also the one who told me Father had made his quick recovery by putting all his own money and much he had from northern investors into buying up land from distressed plantation owners.

I was just the opposite from Bessie. I never knew what was going on.

That spring the doctor, who had at first been quite strict about the dangers of the cough medicine he prescribed for Mama—"One teaspoon only, morning and night"—put the bottle of medicine in my hand and told me I could give her as much as was needed for the catarrh. He seemed to be saying his patient could now swig down all she wanted.

And something else that had never happened before: I heard Bessie argue with my father. "I'm only asking for what's my own back wages."

"If you can't be patient, I can have a darkie in here in a minute—plenty of them down at the Bureau with their skinny hands out. Not another word! You'll be paid in due time."

Around that same time I noticed another strange alteration in our household. I felt my father's eyes pass off the three of us—Mama, Wendell, and me. I knew he was eating most of his meals at the homes of friends in order to spare Bessie. Nevertheless, his absence gave me a guilty relief. I was now able to look after Mama in my own way, and Wendell was allowed to keep to himself, dreaming and singing his silly songs without criticism. Father was busy with business and with Asheville's society. He bought new clothes and hired a team of men to paint our house a beautiful ivory. All summer life had seemed more spacious as Father came and went, spending most evenings helping the Widow Barringer with her late husband's estate.

Mama and Wendell and I ate at the little mahogany card table in her bedroom, at least we two children did. Mama's cough caused her to keep to her bed most days. She would sometimes doze off, her head dropped back on her little baby pillow, the fork still in her hand.

"I am sleeping my life away," she wailed yesterday afternoon. "I am not taking anymore of that cough medicine." And then she began to cough. And I seized the bottle and the spoon and began to pour her a dose.

"No, no, Victoria. We are going to do something pleasurable. You rush home every day from school, never get to play."

"Oh, no, Mama, I'm quite fine." I rushed to pick up the covers which were sliding off the bed as she put her feet onto the embroidered foot stool. It was strange that the thinner and weaker Mama was, the more excitable and beautiful she became. She stepped off the footstool and with her long black hair still undone walked to the window. Wendell, who was turned sideways in his chair, leaned his head against the spokes in the back, stuck his thumb in his mouth and gazed at Mama. I stared also as she looked out at the ginkgo tree in back of our house, the afternoon sun shining through the folds of her lawn nightgown in such a glowing way as to make of her little body nothing but a wispy shadow. She was smaller than me now, and I could no longer wear her hand-me-downs.

"Just look at it, Vic," she said. "Look at the sun on those yellow leaves. If only I could paint! You could do it with your watercolors. The world is so unspeakably beautiful! We are going outside today. Winter is coming, and we must seize this sunny day."

"Please, Mama, come away from that drafty window before you begin to cough."

"I don't wanna go." Wendell said.

"It's chilly outside," I said, "the middle of November. I would never forgive myself—"

"I will be fine. I am getting better. I surely am." She turned slowly like a doll on a music box, her arms outstretched.

"Your arms look like twigs, Mama," Wendell said.

"So they do," Mama replied looking at her arms as though unfamiliar with them.

Wendell slid out of his chair and started for the stairs. By this time of the afternoon, his little room was warmed by the sun, and he would sit in the patch of sunshine on the floor and move his little horses around.

I dressed her warmly—flannel petticoats, muslin camisole, serge jacket and skirt, a heavy shawl, bonnet and gloves, wool stockings and her low-heeled boots. Over my arm I carried the tartan and the feather bed and Mama hugged her little pillow. She'd had this little pillow all her life. Her own mama had stuffed it with cotton and made a little pillow slip embroidered all over with blue forget-me-nots and violets made out of French knots and put it in her cradle. It's all faded pinky gray now but Mama says the little pillow just fits at the back of her neck when she's trying to get to sleep. I notice she also hugs it to her when she's trying not to cough.

Exhausted from the effort of dressing, she rested her arm on my shoulder, and I walked her out the front door and around the yard to avoid the steep back steps. I spread the tartan on the ground beneath the ginkgo tree, and Mama lay down on her back gazing up through the yellow leaves. We loved this—looking up the tree. Even in winter Mama loved the patterns the black branches made against the sky. "See darling how straight out the twigs grow." And I did see them jutting out like thorns or nails. In spring we'd watch for the buds to come on, and on a summer evening lie here to catch the breezes which swept down off the high meadow behind the house. Sometimes, after the sun was long gone but before the stars came out, I would feel quite sure Mama saw something I did not in the tree or the sky, for her eyes would look quite lively as though following a speeding image beyond the branches.

This afternoon I put the pillow under Mama's head and spread the feather bed over her. She lay still, and I knew she was trying not to cough after the exertion of the walk. I crawled in under the feather bed and laid my arm over her waist, careful to avoid the sore spots. As though to welcome us the tree suddenly danced with a great shower of falling yellow leaves. "Oh my!" Mama exclaimed. "How lavish the Lord is! Like golden coins slipped from the Maker's hand."

Lavish, yes, and yet today, I felt the waste of it. So many times I had studied a single ginkgo leaf, holding it in my palm or up to the sun to see beneath the surface the hidden red flecks rushing up from the stem. These leaves seemed made of the thinnest leather like fine kid gloves. Little fans with cunning deckled edges. And with each gust of wind, a thousand more were spilt upon the ground to rot.

"Victoria," she began in her hoarse, whispery voice. "I heard the elegant Mrs. St. Pierre downstairs this afternoon."

"Oh, Lordy." I was glad to hear her playful tone.

"Don't you find her," Mama whispered, "a little, shall I say, girthful for a young woman?"

I giggled.

"A little painted perhaps for a Methodist? a touch forward for—"

"A touch forward! Mama, she is a charging bison. Whatever happened to Mr. Pierre? Did she run him out of that big house?"

"Ah, Vic, when Mrs. St. Pierre turned twenty, she began a new life. She sold her farm to a carpet bagger, moved into town, and changed her name. She just refused to be an old maid."

I was astounded. How is it I didn't know this. I would wager Bessie knew this. "Was there a Mr. St. Pierre?"

"Well, there was a peddler."

"Mama!"

"No, no. She didn't marry the peddler," Mama whispered. "This entirely innocent peddler had come to her farm before she moved, and he sold her some shell buttons. She asked him where these beautiful buttons had come from, and he said, 'Ah lady, these buttons come from St. Pierre.' And I suppose she thought it had an elegant sound, and she bought that house on Montgomery Street in the name of Josephine St. Pierre."

"What was her name before?"

"Nettie Crow."

I burst out laughing. "Oh Mama, that's terrible. Nettie Crow!" I hooted.

Mama coughed hard and deep, then rolled away onto her stomach to spit a small pool of blood onto the yellow leaves. She quickly turned the leaves over, so I wouldn't see it. She lay on her back, her pink cheeks blowing up with trapped coughs. I tried to find some serious thoughts to sober both of us. I looked up into the towering tree. A few leaves were still green, here in November, tender little leaves hugging close to the limbs. Ginkgoes are the strangest trees.

"I wish I didn't have to go to school," I said, a tired old subject between me and Mama. "I can do fractions and decimals and recite Shakespeare and the English and American poets and draw the map of the world. And I have read many more books than the teacher. Can't I quit and stay home with you?" I snuggled to Mama's side.

"Not yet, Victoria." Her voice was so soft I could hardly hear it. "And I wish you would bring to your father's attention that Wendell should move downstairs to the second floor this winter. It is too cold for him in the attic with that cough. I mean, bring it to his attention, later on." Mama was staring straight into the sky. "In case it slips my mind," she added.

"Mama, I get into trouble sometimes at school. Drawing the horses I see right out the window. Miss Ernestine tore up my picture, a mare and her colt."

Mama patted my hand. "I have a good horse story, if you want to hear it."

"A horse story?"

"A true one. My best story, and I saved it for you until this beautiful afternoon." She turned on her side and looked at me in that deep way that pulls me into her mind. She laid her head on her elbow and hugged the little pillow like a doll against her bodice. Mama sighed. She was the best horsewoman in the county, and though she had not ridden in some time, her reputation was well established. When she rode, she and the horse rippled over the pasture like water. Father complained that he could hardly drag her to a fancy dress ball, though, of course, when she got there, she was the prettiest lady.

Mama inhaled a shallow breath and began. "When I was eleven years old, living on the little farm in the shadow of the Smoky Mountains—"

I loved the stories that started this way, on the little farm. One time when Father was up north in Richmond, Mama took me on the train back to Avery County where the farm had been, but there was little to see. We found the charred doorstep and some foundation stones. It made me sad that the house and barn and sheds had all vanished from this place Mama loved so well. She stood where the well had been and seemed completely drifted off, not moving, not even breathing.

"Where are the people?" I had asked.

"Why Victoria, you know your granddaddy Samuel fell at Fort Mahone."

"And Grandma Emma too?"

"Oh, no, darling."

"Did she burn up?"

"Victoria, no!" Mama had said as through such a terrible thing could never happen. "We hid in the woods. Just look there how the vines and the grass make it look like nothing happened here at all and look there at the mountains, their peaks and ridges drifting into view then fading back into those wispy clouds, so mysterious. It's all just how I remembered it."

Mama never told me exactly what happened to my grandmother, and I knew it would pain her to be asked, so on an afternoon when Father had called me into his study to adjust the draperies against the setting sun, I stiffened my backbone and asked him how she died. He looked up from the law book he was reading, frowned, and answered, "Hunger." I did not ask him to explain further.

On that trip back to the farm beside the mountains Mama also showed me a giant sycamore tree where she'd had a rope swing with a log seat, the split side smoothed by her Papa. She gazed up into that Sycamore and said, "I'd drag that rope up into another tree and leap out swinging up so high Ma was afraid to look. I was a wild little thing. Ma once said, 'She thinks she's the Queen of Sheba.' 'Naw,'

Papa said, 'She thinks she's the King.'" Mama laughed that day, standing there where her childhood well had caved in and everything else had burned up. She laughed remembering herself as a child.

Now, lying under the Ginkgo tree, Mama was calm again. But shouting coming from the front of the house made us both lie still. It was the house painter, come again about being paid. The last time father had threatened to take a rifle to the man, but this time Bessie had to handle things. Mama looked as though she had decided not to hear the row and gathered up a little breath to go on with her story. "We had a fenced-in back kitchen garden," she said, "where we hung the clothes to dry. Ma and Papa and the hired help had gone into town one day. I stayed at home to do up my pa's shirts. He said my ironing was the best anywhere around.

"I was laying his shirts across a line when suddenly, like a cloud passing off a mountain top, an Indian boy on a pinto pony appeared at the break in the rails of the fence where I should have closed the gate after the others left."

"Were you afraid of him?"

"I don't think so. He didn't ride in, just waited there framed in the gateway. There were always Cherokees around our farm. Papa traded with them. He said they had pure blood and had escaped the Federal men who forced most of the Cherokees out to Indian Territory long ago. Indians would come to our gate in the morning and wait for Papa to go out to them. Ma didn't like that. 'Why don't they come up and knock on the door like respectable folk?' she'd ask.

"'They are a defeated people, Emma,' Papa would say. Starting as a tiny thing I would go out with Papa and stand, my arm around his leg, while he silently bartered as though he'd turned into an Indian himself. He'd give the leader a respectful nod, and then make another nod to the horses if they deserved it. But if some rag tag heathen showed up with an old nag, Papa wouldn't even give him a nod. He'd start out the door, see the sway back or the knocked knees and turn right back into the house.

"The Indians usually had very fine horses, like this pinto pony. The boy was about my age, sitting there bareback and naked. He sat his mount straight as a pine, and the little pony stood on perfectly straight legs beneath a wide chest—a good galloper. I could tell.

"The Indian boy slipped down from the pony and stood a step away holding the rope bridle in his open hand, so I knew right away that he was offering to trade, and the very idea of me being picked to trade for a horse puffed me up so's I could hardly keep my feet. The boy wore a little a loin-cloth and didn't move or speak. He didn't boast of the pony the way a white man would, pointing out the wide nostrils or bragging about the bloodline or saying how gentle or spirited the horse was. He just stood there like a statue, the rope in his open palm.

"The pony was what it was, a perfect creature. I wanted it like I'd never wanted anything in my life. But what did I have to trade. I thought perhaps the Indian boy had come to our garden because he'd seen our giant pumpkins. Reaching in under the huge prickly leaves I got my arms around one of the bigger pumpkins and looked back at the boy who was staring straight ahead with no interest in me my pumpkin offer. I don't know how he kept from laughing at me, this girl trying to trade pumpkins for a horse. Then I saw his eyes move to the clothesline where my papa's beautiful white shirts hung. I ran to the line and carefully took down the oldest of the shirts and held it up so's he could judge my mother's fine needlework. To my delight he reached out for the shirt with his free hand, and I thought he would hand over the rope to me, but he laid the shirt across the back of the pony and resumed his statue-like pose.

"Well, of course, I said to myself, a horse for one worn shirt. That wouldn't be a fair trade. I ran into the wagon shed and brought out a shovel, a hoe, a bucketful of seed corn, but he wouldn't reach out for any of these. His eyes stayed on the clothesline. I didn't want to part with one of the newer shirts, the one Papa wore to market, but I did and it was laid on the back of the horse, as was his Sunday shirt and finally the one Ma had just finished for him to wear to see the banker in Asheville. All the fine white shirts were gone and still the Indian boy would not hand over the rope. He glanced at the laundry basket, but he could see it was empty. Oh Vic, I don't know what possessed me to be so high-handed with my pa's clothes, but I was still so greedy to have that painted pony, I ran back into the shed, pulled up my skirt and untied the waist string of my best petticoat. The Indians respected fine needlework, and there was nothing to compare with this. Above the tatting on the hem my mother had embroidered buttercups in bright yellow silk thread. No other girl in our little country school had anything like this. I held up the embroidered hem to the naked boy standing not six yards away. He smiled. Indians don't smile often, Vic. They save their smiles. He handed over the rope and walked away with my pa's only white shirts and the petticoat it had taken Ma weeks of working by lamplight to finish."

I didn't breathe, waiting for Mama to tell what happened next.

"I led the pony around to the front of the house and tied her to the porch railing so the folks couldn't fail to see her as they drove up the lane. I wanted them to admire her before I had to explain."

"Mama, I can't believe you were such a naughty girl."

"Oh, I was bold—Samuel and Emma's only child. They reared me like a son." Mama's voice broke when she said this last. It seemed to be an idea—to be reared like a boy—that broke her heart.

I leaned over her. "Was that a bad thing, Mama, to be reared like a son?"

"It was glorious." Her hands reached up as though to pull herself into the tree.

"But what happened when your folks got home?"

"Oh, yes." She folded her hands and took up her story. "I told them about the shirts."

"Not the petticoat?"

"You're the only one in this whole world I have ever, ever told about the petticoat."

"But your mother must have missed it."

"Of course, she missed it, but she never said a word. It was my petticoat, after all, and if I wanted to trade it for a horse, then that was my privilege. That's what she would have said."

"And your father?"

"Papa? He laughed. He loved the little pony before he even got up to the porch. He named her Four Shirts."

I looked down at my mother's beautiful face. A large ginkgo leaf had fallen beside her ear and she looked like a rosy-cheeked gypsy. "Why didn't you tell me this story before?"

"Oh, it was the sort of thing you keep wrapped up, so it won't fade." She looked at me and reached up to push the hair back from my eyes. "Shortly afterward, Papa joined Mr. William Thomas's Legion to fight for the Confederacy." Mama's stomach bucked again and the coughs began. It was getting colder.

"Quickly, we must go in."

"Not yet, Victoria. Listen to me. Robust though my spirit was, I still *had* to marry a strong man to protect me. But everything is changed now the war's over. You can find a husband who will—" She paused. I looked at her, her blue eyes staring at me, frantic with weariness. "—who will talk with you." I rushed her inside leaving for later the feather bed and the tartan in a growing pool of yellow leaves. "I am getting better," she said as soon as we'd got in the house. "I told your father last night, I expected to be completely well by Christmas."

~ ~

I awoke in the night to the sounds of Mama's coughing and Father's voice. He didn't usually go to her, so I was happy for her. I knew I was supposed to stay away whenever they were alone together, but the coughing and retching grew much worse. He didn't know how to help her—sit her up against the big rolled comforter, give her the cough syrup, tell her to breath very softly. My feet skittered down the stairs, and I stood in the crack of the door to her room. Father was standing beside the bed, his back to me. He held her baby pillow in his hand. All I could see of mother was her white arm hanging from the bed. Without looking, he tossed the little pillow to the carpet. There was blood. Like Jesus' face on the handkerchief, the shape of Mama's mouth was pressed into the blood. He had tried to stop the blood, and now she was quiet. He did not move. I turned and very softly climbed the stairs, my mind a washed slate.

The next morning in my attic bedroom I was awakened before daylight by Wendell's climbing into bed with me. He was the worst bed-fellow in all of North Carolina. Every part of him—knees, elbows, pointed little nose—was as sharp as an icicle, and small as he was, he showed a powerful determination in pushing me aside. Once he had positioned himself in the warm middle of my bed, and I'd covered him up and put my arm over him, he fell immediately to sleep, beginning the whistling little snore that always kept me awake until time for breakfast.

I waited hoping to sleep a little more, and perhaps I did, because all of a sudden I thought it had snowed in the night, unheard of this early in the fall. I was certain if I looked out, I would see a thin coat of white upon the leaves below. Wendell went right on whistling, and I lay still awhile before I realized that the certainty about the snow was owed to my seeing the cross pieces in the window frames and the ceiling lit a blue white light from below.

"Children."

So concentrated was I on the light that I heard my father's voice before I saw him standing in the doorway to this little attic room—a space he had never occupied before. Wendell had wakened with the sound of Father's voice, and his head jerked up to bump my chest. Father cleared his throat. "Your mother passed away last night. You should get dressed." He turned quickly back into the little attic passageway.

Where was she? I must hurry. I stepped out onto the freezing floor. "Wendell, darlin', get up and get dressed." I threw my dress over my head. "Wendell. It snowed. Come to the window and see."

"I don't like snow."

I pulled my shawl around me, and rushed down to her room. It was empty and the bed was neatly made—more sharp and tidy in the cold light than it had been in months. Where had he put her? I ran to the window. There was no box upon a wagon in the lane. "Mama?" I had taken her outdoors and lain her on the damp ground. I, her strict little nurse, was in charge of the whole house, and I had not prevented this! Mama, I am so sorry!

I stepped toward the bed. Blackness rose within me, and for a moment I saw nothing. I took hold of the bedpost and hoped I was dying, but the dark faded. I covered my eyes against the morning light. How would I possibly get through one day without her, my only friend.

Down in the kitchen Bessie stared at me through her frizzy hair, her mouth chewing the air. "She was alive. Jesus, Mary and Joseph, I swear she was alive when I came downstairs. Why, last night, after you was asleep, she commenced dancing around the bedroom making plans for Christmas. Your father grabbed her and heaved her back on the bed. I sat with her after he went out. She was alive when I came downstairs. I swear to you, Miss."

"Why didn't you call me?" I wailed.

"I didn't know. Your father found her when he came back around midnight."

"But *then*, why didn't you call me *then?*"

"He weren't ready to tell ya, Miss."

"Where is she?"

"Mr. Riley, the undertaker's got her."

"Why! Surely it is my place to—" Mr. Riley butted into every family's business. I'd seen him slithering along the wall in his plain black suit, fussing with flowers, even touching the body during the viewing, adjusting this or that so everyone would know it was his work that lay at the center of attention. There was not a man in town I found more odious or more unnecessary. Bessie had turned away, hard intent on scrubbing the skillet. Outside the snow was melting noisily, running off the roof and gurgling in the gutters.

Mama had told me of preparing her own mother for the grave, washing the body and winding it in the muslin and helping to lay it in the pine box. She said it grieved her that her Daddy had been buried where he fell at Fort Mahone, and that she had not been there to make sure he was treated tenderly. And now my tender mother was left alone to the cold hands of Mr. Riley. I sobbed and gasped.

"She'll be back." Bessie set a platter of biscuits on the table. "We're going to lay her out in the dining room. You go in there and see if it's like you want."

Like the report of a rifle a knock came at the kitchen door. Bessie let in a tall, gangly boy who whispered something to her. She rushed to my side, her eyes shining so I thought she would tell me Mama had revived. I'd heard of such things, people put into the coffin before their time.

"Mr. Riley has had the most wonderful idea."

"What?" I glared at her through my watery eyes. "Tell me. If it's such a grand idea."

Bessie glanced back at the boy, then said, "He wants to lay her out in her wedding dress."

"No. She should wear black. The Sunday satin."

"But just think of it, Miss Victoria, how she'll look. Thirty-three is not so old. Her hair has not turned."

"But, her wedding dress, surely, Bessie, something from a joyous occasion—"

"It's done, often. I've heard of it, when the woman is not old and sometimes even when she is. Mr. Riley says there is nothing more romantic than the death of a beautiful woman."

"I believe it was Mr. Edgar Allen Poe who said that."

"And surely *he* was a great man."

"My father would never approve." This said I turned and left the kitchen.

I found Wendell way down at the foot of the bed so small and hidden by the blankets that anyone else looking into the room would have thought it empty. I pulled him out. He had wet the bed, and the yoke of his nightshirt was damp with tears. He kept his eyes closed, pretending to be asleep, even when I had stood him up on the floor to peel off his wet things. I dressed him and brought him down to the kitchen stove. Blue under the eyes, he looked no bigger than a three year old.

I had heard Mama bring up Wendell's health with Father long ago. "You've made that boy weak," Father had answered her in a way that made me sure this was not a new topic between them. But surely now he would rush to prevent another terrible loss to our family.

∾ ∾

Bessie, behaving as though a Christmas tree were being decorated for my benefit, did not permit me to enter the dining room until Mr. Riley had finished his work and left. Bessie stood in front of the doors and from her apron pocket handed me a pair of scissors. "Snip a lock of her hair. You'll wish you had." Then she pushed back the doors. "Come and see, Miss."

The draperies were closed, but I could see the dining table had vanished, and all the chairs stood along the walls. A stiff doll lay on the black draped cooling board, a doll in a white georgette dress, which was arranged so that the toes of white slippers showed. Three tall candlesticks burned at the head of the bier illuminating the full, dark hair which was tightly curled like a little girl's. Trailing down with the curls onto the bodice of the dress were thin white satin ribbons. The hands, clasped on her waist, held a small bouquet of Echinacea and ferns. The cheeks and lips were rouged. I tottered and Bessie steadied me.

"Did you ever in your life see something so beautiful?" she sighed, full of gratification for her part in this. Mama herself would have shrieked. She of all people to be dolled up in this cheap fashion. I began to weep again, hot angry tears. There was nothing my mother could do to defend herself from this now. And the opinion that this gaudy exhibit was silly, ludicrous really, appeared to be mine alone. Bessie beside me sniffed.

"You did this," I snapped, "found the dress, helped that awful man."

"I loved her," Bessie wailed. "She was the loneliest woman I ever knew."

I would have slapped Bessie had Mama not been right there. Dear Mama whom I never, ever allowed for one moment to be lonely. Bessie rushed toward the kitchen. I put the scissors away. Mrs. Moody came and took Wendell to her house where she promised to keep him warm until after the funeral tomorrow.

From that point on the day rushed forward at a pace I was never able to overtake, much less gain any control over. Around three in the afternoon a Mr. Frederick, a photographer from Raleigh, appeared and began to set up his paraphernalia, commandeering Bessie to hold up his flares. I didn't know which way to turn. We certainly could not spare Bessie as there were meat tarts, and pies and cookies to be baked and sherry wine and punch and whiskey to be laid out. I did the best I could until some ladies from the church shooed me back into the dining room where I was expected to stand near the door and receive the guests since Father had positioned himself in a chair at Mama's side.

Father's focus after its long absence had returned to Mama, and he propped his elbow on his knee and leaned his head on his hand to gaze at her. At times, his head bowed, his hand covering his eyes. So engrossed was he in her still form, he did not turn when guests arrived to pay their respects but remained part of the candle-lit tableau, shifting only at the prompting of the photographer.

∾ ∾

By eight o'clock the parlor and the dining room were full. Everyone we knew, including girls who used to be my playmates before Mama got sick, as well as many gaping strangers had come, and no one had the decency to go. The air grew quite close and reeked with the perfume Mr. Riley had doused onto the black draperies. The most unwelcome in the crowd was, of course, Mrs. St. Pierre who moved from guest to guest assuring each of her uninterrupted attentions to our family throughout our ordeal. "Such a struggle!" She sobbed. "Everyday my heart was ripped from my bosoms as I witnessed her slipping, slipping—" and then she would dissolve into another round of tears.

The other guests were too overawed by the spectacle of the doll in the wedding dress to pay attention to their role as mourners. "So dramatic," a woman sighed. "Glorious, a real artist," another murmured. But I knew there were many other thoughts abounding but unspoken in the room: *If her spirit is looking down on this spectacle, Margaret Jenkins, who loved things to be plain and natural, will turn over in her grave!* These thoughts sparkled in the air, and their purport was telegraphed to me in long looks and raised eyebrows. I overheard one woman to say, "Oh well, she is too thick to wear it." With this I knew it was believed that the wedding dress had been the silly daughter's idea.

It seemed heart breaking to me that all the thoughts in this room whether complimentary or critical were about the work of Mr. Riley. But when Mrs. Blanchmore, the minister's wife, arrived about half past eight, this changed. In her severe black serge dress, she moved slowly from one guest to the next, putting her arm around a shoulder or waist and murmuring sweet remembrances and pitiful observations about my mother's suffering and courage until tears had been coaxed down the cheeks of her subjects and the faces reddened with grief. "God gathers the tenderest flowers." Then Mrs. Blanchmore moved on like a toy maker turning the key in the back of each guest until she had the whole room wound up and wailing. And when someone asserted their dignity and composed themselves, she returned to give them another twist.

The dark gushings of my mind about my responsibility in taking her out of doors had to stop. So enormous was my own pain, I knew I must exert all my will power to prevent one tear from falling in front of this company, else I should burst into a frenzy that would not do my mother proud. I would be a calm lady and a support to my father.

Although I felt an almost overwhelming resistance to doing so, I went to stand behind my father and look down upon my sleeping mother. By force of habit I watched for the uneven rise and fall of her chest as I had so often when sitting beside her bed. What wretched regrets must haunt my father who had left her alone so much. The muffled weeping, sniffing, clucking, and moaning of the guests behind us swelled as I raised my hand to lay it on Father's shoulder. He turned with a smile, but, seeing it was I, his face fell and for a moment I wondered who he had expected to touch him.

"We must take good care of Wendell," I whispered. "And move him down to the second floor."

Father stood and, taking me by the arm, ushered me into the back hall.

"Victoria, this is not an appropriate time to discuss domestic arrangements. Nor is it your place to make such a suggestion."

"I promised Mama."

"Your mother would want you to hold your tongue."

"She told me—"

"Your mother died of consumption. Wendell has nothing but a bad cold which he will get over if he isn't coddled and treated like a baby girl all the time."

The flood surged. "Father please, I will do anything—" At that moment he drew me to him and began to gently pat my back.

"Ahh," Mrs. Blanchmore cooed from behind me. She was standing in the doorway. "There is no comfort like Daddy's shoulder." I pulled away and ran up the back stairway. I paused at the top, my head about to explode. I didn't move until the pressure and roaring subsided, and I could hear the ladies from the church in the kitchen washing the punch cups. I went into the big bedroom and splashed water on my face.

As soon as I was composed, I took the back stairs down and was surprised to see Mrs. St. Pierre and Bessie standing silently at the bottom as though my approach had interrupted their conversation. I passed coolly between them, but as soon as I was out of their sight, I stopped and listened, not at all surprised to hear angry voices rise up. They had had words several times before. Bessie had once said to me, "Mrs. St. Pierre is nothing but a farm girl like meself."

Now I heard Mrs. St. Pierre rasp, "You might lose your position very soon."

"Don't get your hopes up, Miss Crow. Mr. Jenkins has promised Mrs. Barringer a honeymoon Caribbean cruise."

I heard the pop and knew that Bessie's cheek was stinging. Mrs. St. Pierre, a wild, lost look on her face, burst from the back hallway toward the dining room almost running into me. She rushed past my father who gave her puffing exit no notice, and I realized at that moment that he knew little of the dramatic effects he had on the lives of others nor did he care.

I followed Mrs. St. Pierre into the parlor where her eyes cast about at all its fine things and all its fine company. Her mouth open, she turned, round and round, like a leaf riding into the gully. I strode past her to open the front door for her though I'm sure she believed it was a spiteful act. I understood her shock. I too felt myself winded. *Mrs. Barringer, a honeymoon Caribbean cruise!* Bessie would not have made that up. It was too extravagant, too horrid a story to be concocted by the likes of Bessie who craved the details of the true world.

I returned to the upstairs room and looked down into the yard where I had let my mother lie on the damp ground, the very worst thing for her. And just as I realized I would have to carry this heavy knowledge locked inside me for the rest of my life, my heart sagged further under thoughts of the plans my father had clearly made before my mother's death. I bowed my head against the cool window glass, as the dark suspicion ran through my veins, something more I could never speak of.

Setting the lantern on the floor in front of the empty fireplace, I pulled out the bottom bureau drawer and removed the wedding photograph. I sat a long time staring at the strong, handsome man and the girl trying to say something. After awhile I began to feel happy for her, this bride. Her only daughter had grown old enough just in time to understand what she had said: *... find a husband who will talk with you.* I got to my feet, took a pair of scissors from the table and cut the picture in half. Then holding a corner to the lamp's fire, I set my father's photograph ablaze and threw it in the fireplace. As I watched the edges curl and his face darken, I was drawn to a distant pounding outside. I looked through the moist pane which gave a view of the ginkgo tree now mostly bare and black against the sky. Its arms framed the moonlit horizon where a girl rode astride over the meadow, flowing with the freedom of rushing water, moving as one with her pony.

THE END

THE DRESS
1970

Since Margaret's wedding in North Carolina in 1870 the pounding hearts of all the brides who faced the mirror standing on the little embroidered footstool resided in the heart of Patricia, the newest bride to step up and look and wonder what she has gotten herself into.

My best friend, Sandy Zotikos, and I deplaned at Will Rogers Air Field in Oklahoma City on August 6, 1970, the day after Congress adjourned. My parents met us at the airport and we drove south to Chisholm and the house where I grew up, a nice old place, built by my great grandfather, James Eliot Hale, to which my parents had through the years made improvements—enclosing the old back porch to make a laundry room, adding a bathroom upstairs, replacing the rickety old garage with a car port.

As we headed for Creek Street, Sandy, my wiry-haired, big-voiced friend from the Bronx, kept asking questions—

What's the payroll around here? Is this a union town? Her questions and my parents' bewildered attempts to answer continued until we drove into the driveway. My father opened the trunk, set our bags in the shade of the carport, and jerked his head toward the back of the house. "I've got something to show you," he said.

That was the first time I realized that the light around our house had changed. The house and the old pecan tree poked up sharply into the big, blue sky, the setting so stark I thought for a moment my father had moved the house to another neighborhood. As we rounded the back corner I saw that the cool, deep shadows of the orchard behind the house had been totally wiped away—all the hiding places; the perches from which we cousins had bombed aircraft carriers and Tokyo; all the safe harbors; all the secret bowers—gone.

I stood still as a banker gaping at a ransacked vault.

"What do you think?" my father prodded. "How does it look?"

It looked immaculate, a carpet of green as even in color as the rugs used to hide gravediggers' mounds from the mourners. It stretched from the foundation of our house straight back to the curb of Washburn, the next street over—a small area really, nothing but one lot behind our house, not the vast wilderness I had explored as a child, just a long, green rectangle.

"Once I got all the stumps out I was able to bring in a back hoe and a dump truck," he said. "Remember that big caved-in spot behind the old garage, that old root cellar, a hole I could never fill up before? Stoop down and look." My father demonstrated by squatting and laying his head close to the ground. "Absolutely level."

Finally, I was able to say, "Looks like a putting green," and that seemed to satisfy him. He turned back toward the carport to collect the luggage. Mother and Sandy were standing near the back door staring at the flood of green. Daddy would probably want to show this to Josh.

"So what happened to the hundred-and-sixty acre claim?" Sandy asked Mother, a plain question, an obvious question, one I'd never voiced.

"Cecil joined the army as a second lieutenant shortly after we married, and we moved to Ft. Dix in New Jersey. When we came back for my father's funeral, these two lots were all that was left."

A relative or a friend would have said, "Oh well," and quickly moved to a more felicitous topic, but Sandy made no gracious covering murmur.

My mother, a woman who could always slather incompetence, disappointment or agony with gooey praise, rushed on to say, "My father was very generous, helping all his family, especially my mother's younger brother Wendell who tried to start up a chicken farm with a whole processing plant." Mother laughed her mirthless, phony laugh. "Neither one of them knew much about chickens or business. Wendell died of influenza." Mother turned away from the flood of green. "There used to be a creek out front, right where the street is now."

∾ ∾

"What a practical dress," Mother said when I showed her the short, nylon navy shift I was going to wear to the bridal shower. "You can dress it up or down." Then she proceeded to bring me an array of pearls, pins, necklaces and scarves with which to lift the first dress I'd bought in years to the highly accessorized level of her friends.

Mother was a lovely lady who managed a difficult life by keeping the surfaces smooth. This was going to be pulling teeth for both of us. I believed the wedding itself was a concession to my parents, that my coming out here to tie the knot in the family church should be enough to make my mother forget a few of the details. She obviously assumed that I, having been the dutiful daughter all my life, would naturally fulfill all the bridal roles my younger sister, Olivia, had escaped when she convened a hasty nuptial in a cow pasture and ran off to live in a rural commune. Since that rustic occasion, there had been intermittent pressure on me to redeem the family image.

∾ ∾

That night Sandy and I slept in my childhood bedroom, under the roof on the shady side of the house, Sandy occupying the twin bed formerly slept in by Olivia. I did not sleep well. I tried to fantasize about Josh and me tumbling around on our mattress in the shelter of the grand piano but I felt dull, not like the funny, sexy woman Josh had fallen in love with. Something had happened when that Oklahoma heat hit my face as the door to the plane opened. Except for short Christmas visits, I hadn't been home since graduating from college.

1970 was not a good year for peace—either in Vietnam or on the home front. In Washington I fought hard on the war issue as a lobbyist employed by the Council for a Livable World—a venerable organization started in the 1940's by a Hungarian atomic scientist who had worked on the Manhattan Project. Through the years the Council had become part of the American Left establishment, focusing on arms control and other issues of world peace. In the past year we had put together some good votes for peace and reason in the House and the Senate, but Nixon won all the big ones.

Since the first of the year a bunker mentality had reigned in our little office near Capitol Hill. I loved it. I was the person I had always wanted to be. The one with the fast comeback or the wink that made the gang laugh. We worked nights and ate hamburgers while we poured over the *Congressional Record*, Pentagon briefings, treaty protocols. We only stuck our heads out to shower and change clothes if we had an appointment with a congressman or his legislative assistant. I would put on my one dress; each man would put on his one tie. We wanted to look respectable and respectful. But back in the office we were ostentatious in our lack of grooming. No decent peace activist shaved her legs, and this summer, when we began to go sleeveless, the other females—Sandy, as well as our secretary and the college interns—made it clear underarm hair had become an emblem of political sincerity, identification with the Third World, and rejection of the false values of our mothers. And so with stomach-knotting ambivalence I, the scruffy, nearly thirty-year-old political activist, had to clean up in order to go back to Oklahoma to get married.

~~

I lay in bed the first morning home listening for the birds in the orchard which had waked me throughout my childhood. But the orchard was gone, replaced by a meaningless rectangle. What I heard instead was the rustle of tissue paper. Sandy, who'd made an early start on her two packs a day, was puffing away and wrapping her shower present.

"What is it?" I asked.

The cigarette dangling from her lips, Sandy kept her square body between me and the gift.

"You better show me," I said raising my head

"Oh, no." She gave me a leer of sexual mischief.

Mother poked her head in the bedroom door. "I've made you girls appointments for hair and nails this morning."

"Oh thanks, but no thanks." I said letting my head drop back on the pillow.

"Sandy? Shampoo and set?" Mother asked.

"Guess not. I'll just give it a shake." Like her political opinions, Sandy's curly hair bristled, a Greek girl's Afro. She stood beside my bed, short and stout, a hedgehog between Mother and me, my buffer. I couldn't have faced the wedding without her.

Mother inhaled a cheerful, "Okay," and went off to cancel the appointments. I didn't want to be peevish. But just being in this house, breathing the close, August air, made me clench my teeth. It would have been nice to fulfill all Mother's wedding fantasies, but too much pretending would enrage me.

Josh and I could have held the wedding in Washington, of course. Our friend Moh Chatah, who owned the club where Josh played the piano weekends, offered us everything—the room, the food and drinks.

"Do you really want to go back and get into all that?" Moh had asked, his luxuriant black eyebrows and mustache wincing sympathetically as though he'd grown up a Methodist on the bank of the Red River instead of on the banks of the Mediterranean. He knew how weddings brought all the chickens home to roost. But I couldn't imagine my parents eating plates of Kifta Kabobs and drinking Arak in the midst of the gyrations of my rowdy, hairy friends. And to bring a minister—if we could find one who'd marry a Christian and a Jew in a Syrian Restaurant—would have seemed a sacrilege to Mother. I was a little squeamish myself. Better to go home and get this over with. I would tell my Washington colleagues the photographer forgot to load the camera, just to keep down the hilarity in the office over seeing me in a long white dress and matching shoes.

Before I could get out of bed, my father, whom we kids still called The General, came to stand in the doorway and stare into my room with a wistful frown. He wore a crisp sport shirt and creased slacks, ready for any project public or private, that might need taking care of this busy day before the wedding. For a second our eyes locked and I felt how distant and irrelevant he had become, more so even than ten years ago when I had written him off after I saw him on the porch of a shabby bungalow holding a strange woman's hand.

Sandy, still in the T- shirt she'd slept in, stared at her host with no welcome whatsoever in her eyes. He frowned right back. It took me a second to figure out that it was probably not the impending marriage of his elder daughter that caused my father's frown, but the presence of this strange guest named Cassandra who had been sleeping in his daughter Olivia's bed.

Olivia was his favorite. Whenever she was in the room, he could look at nothing else. Until she and I started going on dates I envied all the attention she got, but after I watched Daddy greet each of her prospective boyfriends with his hands on either side of the doorframe as though he weren't going to let them in at all, I became glad he didn't care who I went out with. He always waited up for Olivia and would greet her with some judgment on the guy. "Someone ought to tell that boy to stand up straight." Or if the guy had longish hair, "He'll make someone a good wife."

After an unsmiling 'Hi,' to Sandy, The General pivoted and left. Sandy closed the door. "He does that a lot, just gape into your room uninvited?"

I let out a loud sigh and got up to get dressed.

~

Since we didn't have to begin a long morning of grooming, Sandy and I had time for a leisurely breakfast. We sat at the round oak table in the kitchen drinking coffee and eating cinnamon rolls. Mother had again repapered the walls with a pattern of cups and saucers. No more pink roses. She'd painted the woodwork a slate blue. The table, once pink then white, was now blue also.

My father was preparing to leave to double check everything for the reception downstairs at the church. Mother had done this yesterday, but The General announced this morning he should check the electrical system as well. He was, after all, the city engineer and a former ordnance officer.

I could see him through the music room, standing at the door of the room where my brother was sleeping surrounded by my wedding gifts. Ernest had arrived late last night from a camp in Minnesota where he was teaching portage to underprivileged boys. The vision of thirty urban, would-be delinquents carrying canoes over their heads, trekking through the forests of Minnesota with my tall, bearded brother in charge, made me proud. Ernest was a natural with kids, quiet but firm.

"As the bride's only brother, of course you should help transport the gifts," my father insisted through a crack in Ernest's bedroom door. Ernest's voice came through as a low rumble.

"Okay, then." The General sounded delighted. "Departure at 16:00."

"How the hell does anyone out here know what's going on?" Sandy asked brightly, mashing her cigarette butt on her saucer. She was trying to read the *Daily Oklahoman*.

Mother, always sensitive to comments about Oklahoma, turned from the sink. "Well, Sandy, we have exactly the same television news shows you have in Washington." Thinking this sounded harsh, she added, "I guess. I don't really know what you all are watching."

Sandy, thinking she'd finally gotten into a real conversation with my Mother, countered, "But just listen to this totally biased report of the demonstration at Stanford." She folded back the newspaper in preparation to reading aloud.

"Cut it out, you two," I said. Sandy, who believed mouths were created for argument, stared at me.

Mother looked apologetic. "I bet you girls would like a rest from politics, and I hope this whole weekend will be a lot of fun for you."

~

"Here comes our bride," Mrs. Worth sang out when Sandy, Mother, Grandma Vic and I walked into the shower. Mrs. Worth was the right one of Mother's friends to hold this event. She had a big air-conditioned house, cushy, expensive furniture, and a jolly disposition, which could be counted on to smooth over any rancor on the part of the stingy bride who'd told her mother one bridal shower would be more than enough.

Taffeta slips rustled against nylons and baroque pearls swung on silk bosoms as the guests rushed forward to take my hands. My mother's friends were restrained, gentle of voice, and fragrant with scents that flung me back into church—Chanel No. 5, Estee Lauder's *White Shoulders*. These women didn't feel politically compromised by eye shadow or nail polish, and my first thought was how glad I was I'd put on stockings and lipstick, the better to impersonate the girl they thought I was. I did care about their feelings. I was redeeming not just my family, but my generation. I felt like the only bride in America.

Mother helped Grandma Vic to an armchair in the circle. My grandmother was the only woman wearing a hat. Having been a milliner all her life, she kept up with changing styles, but she was also 96 years old and knew what looked good on her—in this case a fine lavender straw with rose silk violets. She wore an ivory linen dress with lace inlay that could have been a chemise from the '60's or the '30's, but looked perfect on her. In spite of the grinding work and physical suffering of her life, this widow sat erect, maintaining the presence of a grand dame. The netting on her hat trembled with palsy, and she kept both hands clutched on the head of her cane, driving it into the carpet for stability.

Sandy had also bought a new dress for the shower, blue denim in a western motif. She had a natural swagger in her walk, so the fringe along the shoulders and sleeves swung with authority. I believed she sincerely thought when she bought it, that this cowgirl outfit was what Oklahoma ladies wore, and I felt grateful to the other guests who greeted her warmly ignoring the dress and the untamed hair.

Sandy was seated on my right in the circle and given a net bag the size of a pillowslip in which to collect the bows off the gifts. "Jesus, Pat," Sandy whispered looking around at the circle. "I feel like we came here in a time machine. You're gonna help me out, aren't you?" Although her NYU transcript and FBI file gave her stunning credentials in our office, Sandy Zotikos had no experience with this sort of

WASP ritual in which she'd just been given a substantial supporting role. Normally she was irreverent and occasionally coarse in ways that had never bothered me before, but today I hoped that having been an anthropology major, she'd study this tribe and keep her mouth shut.

As soon as I was seated, tradition took over. There were ten minutes of chitchat while I answered questions about my groom and was asked if I had a snapshot of him. I fervently wished I'd had an informal snapshot—one of the ones we took on our trip to Harper's Ferry, for instance, showing a smiling dark-haired guy in jeans whom these women would immediately accept as fitting. But alas, when Mother's phone call came reminding me to bring a picture, the only one Josh and I could lay our hands on was the black and white head-shot Moh Chatah had had made of Josh for the Mediterranean Club's advertising of their jazz pianist. The photographer had achieved the aura of a matinee idol—a dramatically lit three-quarter profile that caught the shadow of his long eyelashes on his prominent cheekbone.

∾ ∽

I fell in love with Josh on our first date, a sunny Saturday afternoon outside the Library of Congress. A group of Peruvian musicians stood in front of the Neptune fountain playing their Andean pipes, a music I always found universal in its simplicity and evocation of heaven. Joshua and I had walked all the way up Capitol Hill from the Tidal Basin, carried along by the fine weather and our excitement over each other. What were the chances of finding someone so perfect! If asked, I would have agreed to walk on to Baltimore, but when Joshua stopped for the music, I felt the tiredness in my legs.

As soon as the first song was over, Joshua grabbed me by the waist and swung me up to sit on a wall by the stairs to the Library. Then he leaned against the wall and folded his arms to listen as the music resumed. Providing me a place to sit on that day was the last thing he ever did that reminded me of my father. The difference was that Joshua then settled down to listen, whereas Daddy would have continued to look for other people he could seat, traffic he could direct, or trash he could pick up. "He's a musician but his day job is compiling data on the bald eagle for the National Preservation Federation," I told the shower guests without much hope of overcoming the lounge lizard effect of the 8 x 10 glossy I released to float around the room to be stared at by each shower guest. A breathy "Oh my," was the most frequent reaction. The truth was Josh wasn't happy at National Preservation. The administration was very bureaucratic. He had felt smothered by each of the organizations he'd worked for.

But none of that mattered now. I wished these women could have just a tiny inkling of the man Joshua was. He always stopped to listen to street musicians and stayed to talk. Besides being a musician, a performer, and an inveterate music researcher, he was like a cheerleader to the guys who worked out in the weather, as though he couldn't get over his good fortune at having a steady indoor gig, not that it brought in much money. I began opening packages.

"Jesus Christ," Sandy whispered, "Sterling silver!" Tense smiles jerked on the faces of Mother's friends, all unused to hearing their Savior's name used this way. "Sorry," Sandy whispered, even more softly.

"Forget it." I lowered my eyes and tore off another ribbon. The opened boxes were passed around the circle: china and silver in the patterns Josh and I had hastily selected; silver and pewter Revere bowls in various sizes; candy and nut dishes; enameled cast iron and Corning Ware casseroles; and stacks of linens for a double bed. I'd forgotten the generous outpouring that accompanies a church wedding. No wonder they used to be so popular.

In addition to having Sandy as my maid-of-honor, I had invited my only sister Olivia, to be my matron-of-honor. But she wasn't coming to the shower. The crease between Mother's eyebrows deepened each time someone asked about Olivia, her life on the commune outside of town, or the progress of her pregnancy. But the pregnancy made a good excuse for Olivia's absence, and Mother could depend on her friends to accept and expand on any story she wanted to tell.

Olivia, who'd formerly had a quick-silver mind, had reportedly dropped out as a thinking individual. On the phone Mother's quavery voice had told me I would hardly recognize Olivia. Then, in customary fashion, she'd back-peddled and said Olivia probably just had the flu. My sister had long held Mother at arm's length, never confiding. Besides, Olivia had no phone. I had called my old high school friend Calinda to find out what was going on. She'd seen Olivia only once in front of a wholesale grocery, wearing overalls, loading a flat bed truck with huge bags of flour, corn meal, and cartons of cheap canned goods. "She told me a fortune teller had said her baby would be a girl," Calinda said. "Other than that your sister can't be counted on for much more than smiling and nodding, and I don't think it's just what they're smoking out there."

Evidently, I shouldn't count on her even for that. Olivia had sent word this morning that she'd just harvested a great heap of zucchini and needed to can it all today before she lost it. Right Olivia, everyone knows how delicate zucchini is.

"Are you going to wear a white dress, Patricia?" Mrs. Ritter asked with an apologetic smile. "I only ask because my own niece got married in her blue jeans." A sympathetic titter went through the crowd.

"White dress, white cake, bridesmaids, big church wedding," Mrs. Worth spoke up with as much pride as if I'd been her own daughter. She knew Mother couldn't gloat, so she, as best friend, did it for her.

Before I got to the bottom of the up-turned white umbrella of presents, Sandy slid out of her seat, retrieved her gift and shoved it under her chair. I frowned at her—what's going on? "Frederick's of Hollywood," she whispered.

Old Mrs. Pryor, invited only because she was the church organist and wedding coordinator, gave me a saccharine smile. "If only the other girls understood the importance of saving themselves for the big day the way Patricia has." Mother, seated directly across the circle, blushed. No one else in this room would have made such a stupid remark. I looked at my watch. The shower was exactly half over. This time tomorrow I would be married.

On that sunny afternoon in front of the Library of Congress I had sat on the wall and stared down at Joshua's dark curls and the nascent balding beneath them, at his heavy eyebrows and lashes, the arc of his thin nose above the long upper lip. For some reason I found the physical space between us thrilling as he stood beside my dangling feet, his whole attention absorbed in the music. This man would never need me to inflate his accomplishments, to flatter and cajole him into being a decent human being. He would be an independent heart, full of an aesthetic song for which my father had no ear. And in the coming year, I would come to find his independence—almost an aloofness—erotic.

Mrs. Worth served *petit fours* and a lovely punch made with ginger ale and lime sherbet. It was light, frothy, and not too sweet. The punch bowl and the silver tray were separated on the white cutwork tablecloth by a centerpiece of pink rose buds. A Sterling silver epergne held mixed nuts. There was a sheen to this style of entertaining that only experience and caring could achieve. Brightly polished dessert forks fanned out between the piles of fresh-ironed luncheon napkins and glass punch cups.

Sandy stood alone near the door to the kitchen in her cowgirl outfit swigging down her third cup of punch. "That's not going to do you any good," I whispered.

"What *is* it?" she asked and laid her cup on a mahogany buffet. The room was full of chatting women, as warmed and exhilarated as though they'd been drinking champagne.

"Is this how your tribe celebrates?"

I raised my eyebrows. "Too sedate?"

"Anthropologically speaking, I'd say, this bunch looks bankrupt. Everybody's so calm, like they've each had a lobotomy. Nobody's giving the bride any advice. No songs, no fertility dance, no beer, no dirty jokes. I'm pretty sure none of these women has ever had sex."

I smiled at her.

"And you. You are unrecognizable. Where's my friend, the sexy little broad who kept her office rowdy? Weren't you the one who stood on her desk and sang "I'm Just a Girl Who Can't Say No" from *Oklahoma*?"

"This is almost over."

Sandy had picked up on the claustrophobia I felt when I was home, but I hoped she'd also get a sense of the goodness here—this perfect white table, these gentle ladies, each keeping her own counsel, each having left experience at home, bringing only best wishes. This was flawless icing over broken cake, our ritual of faith in the power of love.

∾ ∾

The General had pulled the new Buick up under the Worth's carport and was carrying the gifts out the back door even before all the guests had left. His shoulders had rounded just a little since he'd been an ordnance commander during WW II and later when his guard unit was called up for Korea, but his square jaw still pulsed with the readiness for duty. I noticed he'd arrived alone. Where was Ernest?

"Put that stack down, Mr. Brady." Calinda, seated at a desk in the sunroom, spoke with the authority of a woman with an important job. "I haven't finished double-checking those cards." I stepped down the two steps into the sunroom just as my frustrated father's face darkened. Without a word he set down the stack of open, tissue-stuffed, gift boxes and picked up another.

"Nope," Calinda said, "Leave all the rest of these. You've already taken the only ones that can go."

My father puffed out a breath. He was unaccustomed to being spoken to so brusquely. This was painful to watch. I had thought I had no sympathy for him, but I guess I did. As I stood there, saying goodbye to my mother's friends, I realized that I'd never told my father anything of importance, especially about any trouble in my life. Aware of how he reacted to disorder, I took any prickly problem to my mother. Olivia and Ernest had done the same. And she probably hadn't been all that willing to share the precious confidences we brought her. So for gratification my father had only the steady accomplishment of the tasks he assigned himself.

Mother had been back in the kitchen with our hostess and now she rushed out to the sunroom. "Oh, darling, I'm so glad you're here," she said, giving him a pat on his militarily braced shoulder.

"Hello, Cecil," Mrs. Worth said. "Don't you look nice. Would you like some punch and cake while you wait for Calinda? She is the most conscientious recorder I ever saw. Patricia will be able to thank all the right people for their gifts."

"Come on into the kitchen, Cecil," said Mrs. Ritter. "There are cashew nuts. I know you like those."

Oh, good grief! My sympathy for him vanished. Did he have any idea how they managed him?

~~

"You missed an other-worldly experience," Sandy said to Ernest who was sitting at the breakfast table when we came in the back door laden with packages. Well over six feet tall, lean, broad-shouldered, with massive, flying hair, untrimmed beard and tiny wire-rimmed glasses reflecting the afternoon light, my little brother Ernest looked like an old Bolshevik. He was a senior in college, a quiet organizer who'd led numerous demonstrations on the Swarthmore campus and who'd gone door to door for Gene McCarthy in '68.

He eyed the door to see if The General was behind us. "I was dis-invited," he whispered and rose to help with the unloading. Tension paved the driveway as Sandy, Ernest and I, under close supervision, emptied the car. We carefully stacked the boxes under the dining room table and in the corner by the hutch. The table itself was already covered with unopened boxes from relatives, friends, and civic colleagues of my father. After Josh arrived, he and I would open these.

Sandy, Ernest and I sat down at the kitchen table. Outside the window a plume of water rose from the hose. The General had polished the Buick early this morning, but he would rub it now over and over until he felt better.

"Do I want to know why you got dis-invited?" I asked Ernest.

"Suffice it to say there is no way in this house that withdrawal from Vietnam can be interpreted as a courageous act. I tried to tell him McGovern-Hatfield wasn't traitorous."

"You filthy pinko," Sandy said.

Ernest leaned back in his chair to bask in the older woman's praise.

"Are you going to be okay with the tux?" I asked.

"You're the boss."

"Look, if I can put on high heels, a long white dress, and lipstick, you can—"

"Patty, this is not a problem. The tux will be my cover. People will think I'm President of the Young Republicans." He grinned then dug a note out of the pocket of his jeans. "Incidentally. A guy called and wants you to know he's arrived and is sacked out in the motel."

I jumped up, grabbed my purse and headed out the back door. "Daddy, I need the car. Josh is here."

"Good," he said, rising from polishing the mirror on the driver's side. "I need to talk to him." He opened the car door.

"Maybe tonight at the rehearsal dinner."

"No, I'll go now. He's at the Sooner Motel?" He got in and started the car.

"Daddy! He's not expecting you. Please don't. This is my fiancé!"

"And I haven't even met him!" he said, revved the engine and backed away.

"Daddy! Stop!"

∞ ∞

The groom, an only child, had lost both parents in an accident when he was in college. And because his best friends were all musicians, unable to afford a flight to Oklahoma, he was borrowing Ernest to be his best man. So, when Josh showed up that evening at Deschner Memorial Methodist Church for the rehearsal, he was a man traveling light. A condition I secretly envied. I ran toward him as he and the General got out of the car in front of the church. The limber, dark-eyed musician, his coat flapping in the wind rushed toward me. The stark contrast between him and the buttoned up soldier-engineer, thrilled me. I threw my arms around my groom—slim ribs, the smell of Dial soap, the bluish cast to his well-shaven chin—I felt home again. With the General closing in behind him and Mother and Ernest stepping out of Deanna's car behind me—Josh didn't give me a real kiss, just a quick, warm nuzzle at my ear.

"I was a little shocked when your father showed up," he whispered.

"Sorry about that."

"We had a good talk."

"Yeah, I'll bet."

"No," he said. "We connected at little."

"What on Earth did he say?"

"He said he'd been lonely since Ernest left."

"What! He and my little brother have *never* had one intimate moment together unless it was the day they took a canoe out of our upstairs. Ask Ernest."

Josh shrugged. "He told me about the time you made a mud pie for him."

"When was that?"

"He said Livvie was just an infant, so you were two or three. He said you wanted him to take a bite and he did."

I would have argued, but Mother was waiting.

"Mother, this is Josh."

She stepped forward to extend a trembling hand. "How do you do, Josh. We're so glad you're here."

"Well, I figured it wouldn't be much of a wedding without the groom." We laughed.

"We've heard only the most wonderful things about you from Patricia."

"Ah, well," Josh replied, holding Mother's hand, "time will straighten out all that." And then they paused, holding hands—the orphan and the most selfless mother in the world. And I stopped breathing, sorry, so sorry I hadn't told Mother more about him. Busy walling Oklahoma off from my Washington life, I hadn't even thought about Mother and Josh becoming close.

I had talked a little about her to him. "She rose from the grave," I'd said one wintry Sunday morning. The jazz brunch Josh played at the Club Mediterranean didn't start till one, and Josh and I had been lying awake sleepily murmuring to each other on his Madras covered mattress half under the grand piano in his studio apartment. "Finally given permission by God, Mother went out, got a job, and prepared to divorce her husband, but then before she could go through with it, she felt God rescinded the permission. She's amazingly strong, but she uses that strength to hold herself in."

Josh had risen up on his elbow and stared down at me. "You've got to give me the details on this, otherwise I won't know your family."

But I didn't want him to know us that well.

ꕥ ꕥ

My matron-of-honor, Olivia, skipped the rehearsal as well. I hadn't seen her since her wedding last summer. What a mess that was! I had rushed home from Washington, and we all hauled ourselves out to this cow pasture in the August heat. The stench. The flies. The groom, a jerk with no identifiable politics beyond growing a filthy beard, made no effort to be gracious to our family or worse, tender toward the bride. My first thought was that she must be pregnant, but that was a year ago, and she was only three months along now.

Actually I was glad she was skipping my rehearsal tonight. Such blatant disregard for me, to say nothing of Mother, increased her thoughtlessness, and made it easier for me not to long for her to be here. I had been closer to her even than to Mother. After the War, when we were five and three, when Mother seemed unable to prevent The General from treating us like soldiers, I still had little Livvie. We were alone in the same boat when The General was home between the WW II and Korea.

ꕥ ꕥ

We didn't really have a rehearsal dinner because Joshua didn't have any parents to host it, and Grandma Vic—one of the chief recipients of this wedding—was too frail to attend. Instead of a banquet with place cards and speeches, the family and the grooms' men and the bridesmaids went to supper at the local steak house. But even this modest attempt to bond the wedding party came to nothing. Like a pinball, every attempt at conversation ricocheted off glares from The General or helpless gasps from Mother. A family with a number of things they definitely weren't going to talk about—anything to do with Vietnam or politics or civil rights, the absence of a blood relative who had snubbed us, or the hurt feelings of her parents—we couldn't seem to bring up anything else. We were seated, fed, and out the door in fifty minutes—just as efficient as it could be short of having us file down a cafeteria line, eat standing up and throw away our plates—which I'd always imagined would be my father's idea of how to feed guests.

But he had paid for everything—this dinner, the flowers, the reception—without my ever seeing him do it. And I needed to thank him, this man I didn't like. That woman whose hands he held that day on Kemper Street had liked him and must have looked up to him. Why wouldn't he go to her or others like her, women who would be awed by his being the city engineer, an army officer, a man to whom the city provided a late model car, a man who could explain electricity.

While everyone stood in the hot wind in front of the restaurant saying what a lovely time they'd had, Josh and I snuck behind the air-conditioning compressor, a spot not ideal due to a floodlight overhead. In our first moment alone Josh touched me under both ears with the tips of his forefingers then traced the edge of my jaw lifting my chin and brushing my lips with his. Then he cupped my cheeks in his palms and we kissed, deeply, and my eyes closed imagining ourselves back in Washington, alone. "Queen of my heart," he breathed. I looked into his beautiful dark eyes, as the wind whipped my flowered skirt against my legs.

"I wanted to tell you before tomorrow," he said, "I quit the Federation."

I wasn't expecting this and took a breath before saying, "You did?"

"Yeah, I gave notice. By October I'll be a free man. It was the right time. The Jazz Festival is in October, and it'll make a great honeymoon for us."

"October? The Senate will be marking up the Defense bill right then. I couldn't take off." The June bugs knocked into the lamp above us and fell heavily into the parking lot.

"Ah." He shrugged. "My peace warrior." His gaze was soft, admiring, then he glanced in the direction of the farewells and slamming car doors. "Well, anyway, as soon as I get back from the Festival, I'll get another job. You know that."

"Of course, I know that, Josh." I looked down. The whirling wind pressed the flowered skirt against my legs and swept the dazed June bugs toward the curb.

"It won't be a problem. I've got good recommendations. Maybe I'll find an environmental group that isn't run by Prussians."

"You're an artist, sweetheart. It may take awhile."

"But there's always the job at the club. Moh says I've got a lifelong gig, right?"

"Sure."

"So, you're not worried or anything?"

"No, Josh, no. Of course not. You'll get another job when you get back from the Festival, an event you shouldn't miss anyway. I'm just glad you'll be free to go for the whole thing this time. Then, when you get back—"

"You are something, Patty, the best in the world."

"And the folks at the new job, whatever it is, will be very lucky to get such a smart guy." We kissed again, and I held him and pressed the blue flowers against him.

Back home I rushed upstairs, peeled off my dress and slipped out of my shoes. Sandy, slumped down on the other bed, looked beat. "Pa-at," she wailed, trying on an Oklahoma twang.

"Wha-at?"

"Are we ever going to have a fucking drink?"

I giggled. "I forgot." I pulled my dress back on.

"Forgot?"

"I mean I just kept telling myself I couldn't because I was home. Come on. Let's go to Smokey's and retox."

As we tip-toed past the front bedroom, Mother's voice came out of the darkness. "Pat? It's past 11:00, honey. You're going out? That's fine. Of course. On your way back could you pick up some 2%? If it's easy."

Sandy and I leaned on the bar at Smokey's and each silently downed a mojito. We had almost finished before Sandy asked, "So what's next?"

"A wedding. Two o'clock tomorrow."

She sighed. "The nuptials, themselves, huh?"

"Eternal vows."

"Great." She sounded exhausted, and I knew I'd misused her, pushing her out in front of me, an ill-dressed alter ego. See this, I was saying to the Oklahomans, here is my sole intimate and she is not one of you. Unfortunately my buffer was showing wear and tear.

"Sorry," I said.

"So why are you doing this? Putting yourself through an exhaustive ritual you don't even believe in?"

I took a long drink and stared into that murky mirror that's always behind a bar, so you can keep an eye on yourself. I swiveled to face my best friend. "Sandy, my mother has sacrificed her whole life for all of us. I'm doing this for her. She's thrilled. She told me how wonderful it was for Daddy to be able to invite all the civic leaders and his friends in Kiwanis to a real wedding. To say nothing of his snooty relatives."

"I see. So you're doing it for her and she's doing it for him. Why are you both so nice to him?"

"He needs to feel in charge. I have to pick my shots."

"You passed on the one where he ran over to the motel ahead of you."

I didn't want to think about that scene. "Sandy, we'll live through this."

"He's pulled all of you off track. He's a raging compulsive personality."

"All the more reason to be kind."

Sandy lit another cigarette and blew the smoke above our heads. She swung her bar stool around a few times then rested her arms on the bar. "You know, Pat? You sound depressed. Are things okay with you and Josh?"

"Oh yeah. We've already worked through all our issues."

"Huh?"

"You know, the emotional, cultural, psychological stuff."

"Like what?"

"Well, for one thing, we've decided we don't need to reproduce ourselves. The world doesn't need more consumers, more white westerners who'll use up more of the world's precious resources in one year of their privileged lives than a whole third world village will in a generation."

"Well, thank you for the policy statement."

"Sandy! Population is going to be the biggest issue of our century. Besides, Josh isn't really settled in what he wants to do, besides music, a day job.

"He works at the Preservation Federation, doesn't he?"

"He's given notice."

"When did he do that?"

"Yesterday or the day before."

"He quit his job and then flew out here to get married?"

"Look, Sandy," I swung around to face her. "He wasn't happy there. He shouldn't be doing anything but playing the piano. I love the fact that he isn't a hard charging, go-getter like my father, that he doesn't have to be busy, busy, busy all the time, working, working even when there isn't any work that needs doing, just working because work is all he has. The talks Josh and I have—My parents never talked, not in a deep searching way. Josh and I want to keep our intimate relationship just as it is, not get whipped up into being mommy and daddy, not falling into stereotyped roles, his marching out the door to slave away nine to five."

"But it's okay if you keep working?"

"You know what I mean."

Sandy half laughed and signaled the waiter for another drink. "Boy, good thing you've worked through all your issues."

"What do you care whether or not we have children?"

"Your resistance to becoming a parent might be a little over-determined, don't you think?"

"What does that mean?"

"Well, there's your mother, and then there's your father."

"I just want to get this over and go home. Okay, Sandy?"

"Sure. It's too late to unfuck your life now," she said.

"Go to hell." I whispered.

We sat at the bar without talking. Finally Sandy took a long swig from her glass. "Pat, Josh is probably the right guy for you. I'm crazy about him myself. But when we got off that plane, you turned into a zombie."

Sandy might be right about some of this, but I was feeling disoriented, and I sure didn't need her to stir my anxiety further. All families had problems. We were doing all right.

Mother had worked her way out of depression with the help of her psychiatrist. Ernest had grown into a splendid man of character and good humor. Olivia had chosen a life for herself, and I had found a mate. Only The General had shrunk. I leaned my head in my hands. I should let Sandy drive.

∾ ∾

"Grandma Vic is here, ready to go," Ernest said in the morning when I emerged from the bathroom.

I looked at my watch. "It's only ten o'clock."

"Mom said your flying in at the last minute made Grandma so nervous, she's been running three to four hours ahead all week. She's sitting in the living room."

"Do you think she's bothered by the Jewish thing?" I asked.

"No more than if you were intermarrying with an Episcopalian, which is to say, yes, she thinks it's a shame you couldn't find a nice Methodist boy to marry. She's ninety-six years old, Patty. Mom, on the other hand, is delighted with the Jewish thing—our own bona fide link to the champion underdogs."

I looked at my brother, trying to see his little boy face behind the beard and glasses. "Do you remember the day we took the canoe out of the attic?"

"Sure." A slow grin formed inside his beard. "Happiest day of my childhood."

I smiled back. "I better go say good morning."

In the soft light through the sheers at the bay window my Grandmother Victoria, dressed for the wedding, looked like a faded painting. She had taken off her lace gloves and clutched them on the head of her cane. I moved to her side and kissed her cheek.

"You were my best student," she whispered so none of the generations of other watercolor students could hear her praise me. "When you were a very little girl you had a flare with the brush, a freedom. During the war we had such fun. But then you tightened up, and I couldn't get you to paint the way you had when you were four and five. " She always told it the same way. I inhaled the fragrance of her Madame DuBarry face powder. She squeezed my hand, but kept her eyes to the floor. Her chest rose and fell uncertainly.

"How's your angina?" I asked.

She didn't answer nor did she look up. Suddenly, I knew. It was my Mexican wedding dress. Late yesterday afternoon before the rehearsal, she'd walked the three doors down the block from her little house to stare at my selection— ruffles of gauzy cotton alternating with wide lace. I stepped up onto the tattered embroidered footstool that had belonged to Grandma Vic's own mother in North Carolina. I held the dress in front of my jeans to display it.

"A squaw dress?" Grandma Vic had gasped. She didn't understand why a girl with a professional job in Washington would purchase something so flimsy in comparison to the stiff, satin, stand-alone gowns she was used to seeing the brides of our family zipped into. I'd thought I might get credit for thrift, that being so highly prized in my family, but this morning in the living room her eyes were forced away from me as from one awaiting deportation. I patted her fragile shoulder. "You look so beautiful."

~

Olivia showed up for the wedding, stepping down from a sloppily painted, rusted VW bus into the swirling wind that always encircled our huge Gothic church—a memorial, built by grieving parents in honor of a lost child. I did a double take when I saw my sister carrying her Samsonite Vanity Case and her flapping bridesmaid's dress on a hanger.

"That's Olivia?" Sandy gasped. She'd expected a hippie, of course, and so had I. For some reason, for the first time in her life, Olivia was wearing heavy make-up, a beige mask like something for turning tricks on Reno Street in Oklahoma City. She'd blackened her eyebrows, covered her eyelids with blue grease and painted her full, pouty lips bright red.

"She's never looked like this before. I guess someone who's been living on a commune shouldn't try to jump backward into femininity so abruptly."

When Olivia got sight of me standing beside the entrance, she took a step back. I gritted my teeth. I wanted to run to her and find out what she'd done with the beautiful golden girl my sister had been. But I stood still, and my friend, Deanna, who was approaching from the other direction, her fiery hair flying in the wind, quickly shifted her things into one hand. "Olivia?" she called and hurried up to put her arm around my sister's waist. "Goodness, darlin'. It's so good to see you." She drew Olivia along toward the door. I held it open for them. Women like Deanna were the salt of the earth.

The General had left for the church before I got downstairs this morning. He had announced last night that well before the ceremony he would station himself in the large hallway outside the sanctuary from which he planned to route all the girls—bride, bridesmaids and candle lighters—into the church parlor, and the groom, best man, and the ushers—drafted from the ranks of my cousins—into the minister's study next door.

The church parlor was smaller than I'd remembered, a cloying chamber of flowered wallpaper, flowered rugs and flowered draperies held down by a long dark trestle table. My bridal party seemed to sink into the florid mass. Mother in pink chiffon caught the light, but the bridesmaids and candle lighters wiggling into their moss green linen sheaths became just so many stalks waving here and there amid the flowered upholstery.

Mother was on familiar ground here in the church parlor where she'd called hundreds of meetings to order and bowed her head for a thousand prayers. Dear Aunt Fel was here, her little sewing kit in her purse for any last minute repairs.

The light from the window fell on the huge box left on the long table by the florist. Mother and I approached it. "How're you doin', darlin'?" Mother whispered as we stood side by side to lift the lid of the box.

"Great." We pulled away the waxy green paper and inhaled the fragrance. The light illuminated the wreaths—freesia, baby's breath, and yellow roses to be worn on the heads of the bridesmaids, wrist bouquets for the candle lighters. And one perfect circle of white roses for the head of the bride. Also my bouquet—white freesia, stephanotis, roses and violets tucked here and there. Mother and I had whipped through so many decisions by phone, I was amazed to see these flowers, shimmering before me, evidence of arrangements made and then forgotten. "They're perfect," I said.

She took both my hands. "Oh, darlin'," she whispered, "We like Josh so much—a musician, so sweet and handsome. He's almost worthy of you." She made a teary smile, and I pulled her to me for a squeeze. We both turned to glance at Olivia who'd kept her back to me since coming in. "Please talk to her," Mother said.

"Sure, Mom, I'll find out what's up in just a sec." With my arm around her, I guided my mother toward a corner where we could speak without anyone hearing.

"Everything's okay, isn't it?" she asked.

"Oh course, Mom," I promised, "but I'll be leaving right after the reception, and I haven't had a chance to ask how you're doing, with both us girls gone, and Daddy's blood pressure under control."

Fear glinted in her eyes, afraid I would again urge her to leave Daddy just as I had off and on for the last ten years.

"You're in great shape now," I said, "healthy and working. Ernest off on his own." I held her shoulders and smiled into her eyes. "I want you to be happy, too."

"If you're happy, it will be enough," she said and the worry in her eyes made me feel I had cornered her. She rushed on. "I owe Daddy a lot. I always knew he'd dig ditches for me if he had to." Trapped in gratitude, who was she to complain about a husband who had the one characteristic her father lacked? "Oh Patty, I knew that each of my children would grow up to make good lives for themselves, but you know Daddy." She obviously wanted to stop here, but I refused to nod and make the gracious close. She looked so frantic and sad I really was tempted to just hug her and stop. "You know," she began again, "that he would be lost and helpless if I left."

I saw that I was torturing a woman who didn't have it in her to hurt him. We hugged and then she began to hand out the wreaths. I watched her moving around the room, gently pinning the flowers on all the long hair. I let out a long aggravated breath. This provider business! It seemed so old fashioned—the *male* breadwinner. But her happiness had been my oldest responsibility, and I shouldn't have marred this day for her.

"I have an announcement," Calinda said. "It's been suggested that we remain standing so as not to wrinkle this linen which all of you know won't look like much going down the aisle if we're not careful." Those who had already sat down stood up. Perfume and hair spray filled the air, as these Oklahoma women bent over the mirrors of their vanity cases to arrange their long hair beneath the wreaths. The old pendulum clock on the parlor wall said 1:50. Perfect. The peals of the great pipe organ struck up the introductory music and poured down the hallway toward us. This was the official church organist playing a Bach Prelude. Mrs. Pryor, wielder of considerable political clout in this church, had convinced the minister that as wedding coordinator she should take over the organ when it was time to play the "Wedding March." "That's ludicrous," Josh had said when I told him to expect a shift downward in keyboard skills when Daddy and I started down the aisle.

"Right," I said. "This church has more than one pocket of ludicrous."

Mother returned to the florist's box for more wreaths and bobby pins. I slipped off my shift and laid it out full length on the trestle table in order to fold it. I was aware that Mrs. Pryor, heavy-footed and big-voiced, had entered the room, and my resolve not to acknowledge her drove me deeper into my folding project. She was turning each of the bridesmaids and candle lighters around as though they were little girls whose sashes and pigtails needed tying up. "Better get a move on, little bride," she sang out. "Times a-wastin'."

I threw my full-length white slip over my head and did not emerge from it until she had closed the door behind her. This strapless undergarment to give the dress "a little body," was a concession to Mother who had frowned at my flesh showing though the lace midriff.

Just as I gave the elastic top of the slip an upward yank to settle it snug under my arms and raise its hem off the floor, I realized my error. I glanced about the room where good women were softly laughing and talking, unaware of the bad joke I'd played on us. My face went hot, and I labored to drag in a heavily scented breath as I knocked softly at the door to the adjoining study. To my relief the great dark tree of my brother immediately filled the slightly opened door as though he'd been waiting for my knock, his mass protecting me from view by the groom and his men.

"My dress," I whispered. "It's in a Casa Del Sol shopping bag on my bed." He nodded and was gone. When I turned around all the women were staring at me.

"Don't worry. Josh didn't see me." I tried to smile. In October I would be thirty years old, too old to be superstitious, too sophisticated to believe in accidents.

Mother realized what had happened and turned white. The town would blame her, and The General would blame her, and now she was blaming herself. I rushed to put my arm around her. "Ernest won't be a minute."

A loud knock on the door to the hall drew everyone's eyes away from me. Olivia opened the door, and the organ music swelled in along with my father in his dress uniform. He had rented a tux like the other men. Why wasn't he wearing it? How could he do this to me, make a public display of militarism when he knew damn well I spent every day of my life fighting against this stupid, immoral war!

Sandy stepped to my side. "What is that? He looks like a bellhop at the Ritz."

My father looked splendid. Black coat with bronze oak leaves on his shoulders, his ribbons resplendent across his chest, dashes of red, Persian blue trousers with gold stripes down the sides. White kid gloves. I bit my lip and took in a shuddering breath.

"Where'd Ernest go?" The General demanded of the roomful of women who were fortunately staring at him, so they couldn't see the bride, red-face with anger. "I saw Ernest run out," he said.

"She's not dressed, Daddy," Olivia said, pressing him back and closing the door. The room was silent.

"How can he do this to you." Sandy whispered.

"It's probably not even personal, Sandy. It's probably good for his morale."

She frowned at me. "That's all you have to say?"

"So what can I do? Send him home to change?"

"Oh, he's not ever going to change, but I thought you had."

"You saw him. He hasn't looked that powerful since we arrived. He's happy."

"Jesus Christ, Pat." Sandy left me standing at the window. I looked outside so no one could see my face. I struggled to think only of Joshua, the dearest man I knew, standing on the other side of this wall, good-humored, lending poise to any man in need. This day would end and maybe, twenty years from now we'd laugh about our wedding.

Except for clear-eyed Calinda whom I overheard quietly saying to Deanna—"How many brides have you heard of forgetting their dresses?"—everyone else behaved toward the extremely awkward situation like a proper Oklahoma lady. Part of me wanted to slap each brightly smiling face, but mostly I was enormously grateful to each woman and girl who gallantly pretended nothing was wrong. I sank into a chair.

My thirteen-year-old cousin Marianne had leaned her little bottom against the high arm of a couch and listened raptly while Sandy, the anthropologist, entertained the Oklahomans with her views of men. "Look at them," Sandy was saying, "frail creatures, their most vulnerable flesh riding out in front, just asking for it."

Marianne's jaw dropped.

"Women are the tough ones," Sandy continued. "Look at us, our privates well-nestled in the pelvic cradle, hip bone bumpers. We're the tanks!" she said, slapping the hips of her linen sheath. "Men, poor schmucks, they're the infantry."

"So we need to protect them, right?" Marianne asked.

"You can protect them if you want to," Sandy said and abandoned her metaphor.

Thank heaven, Grandma Vic wasn't in the room. Though she didn't approve of the dress, she wouldn't have understood my leaving it behind. She, who had spent her life having her clothes ready—whatever re-styled, recut, borrowed or rummage sale-retrieved goods they may have been. Out in the sanctuary where one and all could see and appreciate her queen-like appearance, she didn't have to know that her most promising little student was not prepared.

The wreath quivering atop her springy hair, Sandy made her way back to me. She stood close beside the chair where I sat upright in my petticoat. "How's it going, kid?" She was struggling to be kind after I'd pissed her off.

"It's going okay."

"Do you want to marry this guy?"

"I love him with all my heart."

"Well, sure. Who wouldn't love him—the nicest guy I ever met, a musician, perfect for you. But shit, Patricia. You left your God-damned dress behind."

"So?"

"Just checking. One last time."

We both glanced about the tense room then fell silent. No one had made eye contact with me. They couldn't believe what they were witnessing. What I needed was a drive-by rescue. A best old friend? A former lover? Tom? Tom, who would keep the motor running until I got up my courage to walk out of here, hike up this petticoat, and sling my leg over the back of his motorcycle. The thought of the raucous tumbling of his idling motor drew me back to the window. Tom, teller of barnyard jokes. Deanna had found out he was now a negotiator of land rights for Indians in Alaska. Tom, married to a beauty queen, a woman who deserved him. The street was empty except for parked cars.

Another loud knock from the hall door preceded the upper half of my father, bending at the waist as though keeping his feet in the hall meant he wasn't intruding. The organ music poured in, roaring. His face was red and his anger flooded the room like diesel exhaust. "We're thirteen minutes behind! I've sent the groom and his men to the altar!" The room gasped in unison.

"She isn't dressed, Daddy!" Olivia insisted and closed the door in his face. Mother rushed toward Olivia. "Please, Olivia, he's just anxious." My mother's nose was shiny, her face tense with worry. This was the biggest operation for which The General had had responsibility since Korea. Here in the church were bridesmaids and groomsmen, all in uniform. But the operation was behind schedule. I realized I'd been gritting my teeth for some time.

A soft knock came from the adjoining door to the minister's study, and white-haired Rev. Hough walked in, smiling and calm, not a bit deterred by a bride in her slip. "How're y'all doing?" he asked, nodding around the room to each individual. "I guess Mr. Brady told you he sent the boys on down."

Mother rushed to him. "Reverend Hough, we do apologize for this awful delay. I left something at home Patricia needs. Ernest has gone for it. We should be ready to go in less than ten minutes, maybe five."

"Oh don't worry, Mrs. Brady. There's a wonderful breeze blowing across the sanctuary today, and those folks out there are gossiping, having a high old time. A little suspense will only make the wedding more satisfying. Don't mind the time."

"But there's another wedding at 3:30," said Mrs. Pryor's voice from the study behind him.

"Oh," Rev. Hough countered sweetly, "weddings don't take long." He pulled the door closed on himself and Mrs. Pryor. Thank heavens I'd chosen Hough—clearly a failed career, an assistant minister in his sixties—and not Rev. Mapple whose ambition to be a bishop made him impatient with any hitch in the smooth running of his church.

Sandy joined me at the window, leaned one strong arm on the sill, and spoke slowly as though to a stubborn child. "Patty? Weddings are like locomotives—once they've gotten up speed, there's no stopping them, and there's no jumping off. So maybe you want to take advantage here—Remember, you can always shack up with Josh the rest of your life."

I stared out the window and focused my mind on my groom. I loved Joshua's back—the rack of his shoulders, muscled by life at the keyboard, his spine and ribs. On his right scapula were seven small moles in the pattern of the little dipper, one of the few constellations I recognized as a child.

"It's like some sort of marital DNA your kind passes down the generations," Sandy was saying.

"My kind?" I scowled at her.

"You think marriage is about women being kind to men."

"You think that's why I'm marrying Josh?"

Aware that we had everyone's attention, Sandy tried to whisper. "You can't beat this game. It's what you're trained for. Look at your mother."

"And *your* mother is beating the game?"

"My mother's a total loss, and you know it. But you're the genius who left her wedding dress at her parents' house.

You tell me." She glanced at the carpet. Bold and brassy as she was, this was hard for her, standing here in the first long dress she'd had on since her high school prom, bucking the agenda of everyone in the room. "Look," she said, "I'll cover your back if you want to make a run for it, but if you're just toying with these nice people, to Hell with you."

I looked away from her. Josh offered everything—the little dipper, an impressive big dipper, the music.

Ignoring the prohibition against wrinkled laps, Sandy walked across the room, plopped into a deep easy chair, and fished a cigarette and matchbook out of her bosom. I watched my friends watch her. They may have counted on her to talk sense into me. They liked her. I was the one they were fed up with.

Olivia came to my side probably so the room wouldn't have to look at a bride alone in her underwear. It was 2:21. My sister stood between me and the window, her long blonde hair furled outward from her wreath, merging with the sunlight, a halo about her cheeks and shoulders. Yet within this was the annoying mask of her made-up face. I stood and took hold of her slim shoulders and turned her to the light. Under her right eye was a faint greenish half circle.

No! My stomach swerved. Heat shot up my face. Melvin! That God-damned thug had hit my sister, my beautiful, pregnant sister! And she'd been protecting him, staying away from us, ashamed.

I spoke quietly. "You'd rather people think you're a bimbo than have them know your husband is a—?"

"I'm sorry, Patty. I'm really sorry. I tried everything, cucumber, steak. Prayer." She made a sad smile. "I borrowed ice from the neighbors. I'm so sorry." She gasped.

"How'd it happen?"

Sensing an outbreak of emotion, Mother rushed over to usher us toward the door into the minister's study, gently pushed us through, and closed the door. Seeing us, Rev. Hough, departed into the hallway, dragging a reluctant Mrs. Pryor behind him.

The room was large and empty after the crowded quarters next door, and the sunlight streamed in making a glare off the glass top on the desk. Olivia's ravaged face was lit as though she stood by a pond. Alone and free to speak, my sister and I were suddenly shy. I wanted to turn my back, so I wouldn't have to look at her, but I didn't. "Oh, sweetie," I said. "What happened?"

"He didn't want me to go to the wedding. He felt he'd rescued me from Daddy, and now I was running back into the family."

"What? Melvin rescued *you?* Our golden girl, our beautiful tennis player?"

She looked down at her hands and spoke softly. "After you left, I had to get out of there. Melvin was the next guy who asked me out. He hated Daddy. He sided with me. The others had been afraid of him." Then she looked me in the eye. "And for your information," she said, tense, "I was never the golden girl! I tried to make you and Mom think I was. Somebody needed to be having fun. I lived that life for *you*, so you wouldn't think I was strange."

"Olivia. What are you talking about?"

She pushed her full lips forward, a pout that spread into a sobbing mouth. "You don't really care, Patty. You never cared one whit about what was happening to me

"When?"

"When we were little girls."

"Whatever was happening to you was undoubtedly happening to me."

Olivia sniffed. "We shouldn't get into all this on your wedding day, but the answer is, no, what was happening to me was not happening to you. The General never treated you the same way."

"Right. He rarely looked at me, never complained when I changed my hair. He never stopped looking at you."

"He never laid down with you."

I paused and swallowed. Livvie had imagined this, and she was right; we shouldn't get into this on my wedding day. I took a deep breath. "Go on."

She looked down. "He never forced himself into me, Patty, or anything like that. Right after he came back from Japan— I was so afraid of him, really terrified. This huge man who'd left when I was a few days old. He'd just lie beside me looking at the ceiling. Later he started lying on his side, pulling me against him to warm me up."

"God, Livvie. Could you feel—"

"It wasn't incest. Really. He said he'd stay until I went to sleep. It was a long time until I figured out I could just fake sleep."

"Where the hell was I?"

"Right there in the next bed."

"That's impossible, Olivia. Those beds weren't more than four feet apart. How could this happen and I not remember it?"

Olivia shrank under my glare. "I don't know," she said. "You must have heard him. He always had excuses for coming in, raising the window, putting it down, checking to see if I'd kicked off my cover. He was always gentle, not like he was in the daylight, and maybe at first, after a bad dream or something I wanted him there. You and I weren't sleeping in the big bed anymore, and I missed that terribly. Remember playing kitty cuddle?" She glanced up at me. Kitty Kuddle had been the brand name of a soft toy cat she'd had, and that's what she and I called our snuggling down under the covers together, getting as wrapped up in each other's limbs as possible—the softness of flannel nighties, her silky hair—the best remedy for cold sheets or a spanking.

Olivia looked down again. "I probably made him feel I wanted it."

"No! Livvie, don't *ever* think that way." I took hold of her shoulders. "I don't know what to say. How can I remember? I was only five-years-old when this started!"

She gasped and I watched her face twist, the thick make-up melting. "And I was only three."

"I'm so sorry, Livvie." I did remember now a recurring dream I had after the war. I dreamed Olivia was flying, very fast, her pale curls mashed back by the wind. She held out her little arms like airplane wings, and they had fluttering feathers on them. Sometimes she was sitting in the bicycle basket and Daddy was pumping. And it wasn't feathers on her arms. She had on a little white kimono with the long sleeves flying out on either side, flapping as he rode away with her.

I covered my mouth. This was horrible. I had known *something*. Trained as I was in ignoring conflict and denying anger and turning a blind eye on whatever wasn't what Mother would call appropriate, I had suppressed what I knew about my father and my little sister.

I reached for her hands, thick cuticles and snaggled nails from the laundry and gardening on the commune. My little sister. She'd been out on that God forsaken farm, holding borrowed ice on her face trying to heal up so she could go to the wedding of a sister who'd abandoned her years ago to a man who used her, her, Olivia, the perfect little girl. We held each other close for the first time in so long.

"We're going to have to stop," she whispered. " Ernest will be here any second."

"And you never told Mother?"

"I assumed she knew, of course, the way a little kid does. I could never figure out why she didn't come to me herself in the night."

"Livvie, Livvie," I crooned and rocked us.

She sobbed. "You left me, Patty, ran off and had a big Washington career."

I pulled back and looked. Tears had completely uncovered the green bruise under her eye, and the streaming mascara made her look permanently damaged.

"Oh, Livvie, I'm so sorry." We buried our faces in each other's necks. I should have rescued her when I was five, stabbed him with his Samurai sword, then grabbed my little sister and run. "I should have killed him," I whispered.

The door to the parlor swung open. "It's here," Mother breathed. She held up the white, tiered wedding dress.

"I'm coming," I said, but she continued to stand there. "Just give us another minute."

Mother's eyes were wild with disbelief. "Patricia, please. Everyone is waiting."

"Mother. Close the door."

She didn't close the door. Instead she turned to the parlor and said, "She's still stalling."

I whispered to Olivia. "We've got to get you out of that damned commune."

"Not now, with the baby coming."

"All the more reason to run. Mother will help you."

She shook her head. "I've always had to pretend for her."

"It would kill her to know that because she always pretended for us. Come to Washington. I'll take care of you."

The minister's study was filling up with smiling bridesmaids. "Come on, Patty," Deanna said. "Time for the Wedding March."

I let go of Livvie and put up my hands. " Stop! Just give us a minute more here." Mother had unzipped the dress, and she tossed it over my head. I had to catch it before it slid right down the slick petticoat and onto the floor. I pressed my palm to my chest to hold it.

"Oh, Patty," Olivia cried, "just tell me you've got a good man."

"He *is* a good man." Perfect. Sweetest man in the world. And at this moment it became clear that Josh wasn't the problem that had me delaying this wedding. Where was Sandy? She hadn't come into the study with this bunch who were wielding powder puffs and lipstick trying to mend the wrecked faces of the bride and her Matron of Honor.

"I'll be okay." Olivia kept nodding reassurance to me as Calinda attempted to dab cover-up under her bruised eye. "Just you get married and be happy. People can be happy," my sister's voice shuddered.

"I'll zip her up," someone said. "No, I'll get it." "Let Alice have the honor." I looked through the doorway into the parlor where Sandy stood, smoking, looking back at me. Mother put my hands in the sleeves of the dress. I felt the room slide around and wasn't sure where the door had been.

But before Mother could zip me up, the door to the hall opened, and there, the organ music swirling behind her, stood Grandma Vic leaning on her cane, the veiling on her hat trembling. "Patricia!" Her frail voice strained. I dashed to my grandmother. She would guide me out of here. To the rhythm of her gracious, swaying gait, we would leave this church. I looked into her worried eyes.

"Patricia, I've been sitting in the front pew watching your poor groom, and I've come to tell you, I'm afraid he's crying."

Everyone gasped. This couldn't be true. Perhaps she'd seen his shoulders rise and fall as they did in exasperation, but he was an American male and would not let one tear down his cheek in front of a congregation of strangers. And yet her tone was so aggrieved, it forced me to picture him crying unabashedly, his back to the congregation, staring into the vaulted ceiling, letting the tears drain down his neck into his collar—a full expression of grief in rebuke of all these repressed Protestants who, like me, would probably die with a stiff upper lip. God's frozen people.

My grandmother shook with indignation. "Have mercy, Patricia," she gasped. "This delaying is cruel. You cannot do this to a man."

Mother zipped my dress. My little cousin, Marianne, laid the rose wreath on my head. "Don't worry, Patty," she whispered. "All brides have butterflies." Mother, her arm around my waist, escorted me out of the parlor to place my hand in the crook of my father's extended arm. The General took hold of my hand and clamped my wrist under his elbow. Wait! No! I tugged against his grip, but he held fast. Mrs. Pryor lumbered past on the way to the organ. The bridesmaids and candle lighters flowed around us into the sanctuary.

Squads right, squads left.

Although he held me in an iron grip, Daddy was calm now, contained in his dress uniform. From this glorious raiment that set him apart from the civilians in their monkey suits rose the odor of mothballs. I turned my head away, but it wasn't just the mothballs; it was a fresh disgust that put me off. Even the Daddy who had driven me to the church an hour ago *was not* the man beside me now who set his jaw to move forward with this day.

I tried to take deep breaths. My father and I were now to proceed to the back of the sanctuary, but we weren't moving. For some reason he had paused in front of the vestibule's stained glass window—a bird with a branch in its beak. Sandy stood unsmiling beside the doors and watched my father pat his own arm that locked my wrist to his ribs. Though this gesture secured me totally in his grasp, it was probably affectionate. He was looking at me, seeking some gesture reciprocal to his pat, something to reassure him that everything was swell between us, so that he could move on into the abundant glory the rest of the day promised him. And surely, to lay my head against his shoulder or twist my neck to kiss his cheek would have been normal, automatic, my way of telling him this wedding may have had a rough start, but it was on track now, and you, Daddy, you are in charge.

Be nice, Patricia, I told myself. You can't undo what has happened to Mother and Livvie and yourself. Besides, what difference do these gestures make? He smiled, eyebrows up, expectant, asking for a sign, something Mother would have given without thinking—a sweet smile, a gush of flattery—*you look so handsome, Cecil*—these, her well-worn tools always at hand, phony praise to shield him from the knowledge of what a disappointment he was to her. His head was nodding, as if coaxing a reluctant child.

"Josh is a great guy," he said and gave a little shake to the arm that pressed my hand, trying to jiggle out a response. What was wrong with a bride who wouldn't chime in on a compliment to the groom? The organ shifted into a higher, more urgent register; the official organist was still in charge, but my father wasn't moving. It was clear we weren't going into that sanctuary until I smiled at him. "You're gonna to be very happy," he said.

No, I thought. This is not the beginning I want for the rest of my life. I cannot start by marching down the aisle on this man's arm. This would be one more act of pretending, this time before two hundred witnesses.

Be nice, Patricia, the organ pleaded in a high squeal. The hinge of my father's jaw had begun to pulse again. Have mercy. He was begging. My flimsy dress fluttered. Sandy was gone. I wrenched my hand away from his grip and turned to face him, but my knees were snapping backward. The flowers in my bouquet hammered the air. I was falling. "Help!" I grabbed his sleeves.

He grasped my elbows. "What!" He was breathing through his mouth and looked back at the empty hallway. Mother wasn't there to help him. My whole body shook, and he held me up. "What's wrong?" he asked, his voice hoarse. The organ roared. Chaos and disorder. With trembling hands Daddy guided his quaking daughter to the stained glass window and seated me on its deep sill. He glanced toward the sanctuary full of waiting guests. Sweat poured down his temples.

"I need to talk to Josh," I gasped.

My father shook his head, no. I could tell it wasn't *no* he wouldn't go to get the groom, but *no*, this was the last straw from this difficult girl. Why would his sane daughter go crazy today? He started toward the door.

"Wait," I called. "I need to do this myself."

"Do what?"

I rose carefully, and though my ankles wobbled in the high heels, I headed into the cavernous sanctuary at first walking slowly, steadying myself on the backs of the pews. Seeing the bride in the white dress coming down the center aisle, Mrs. Pryor, asserted herself with a sour chord before the "Wedding March" blared forth. The crowd sighed with relief. But this bride was alone, and she was picking up speed. By the time I reached the front pew, I was running. I stopped to whisper to my mother. "I love you very much," was all I said. If she looked at me with confusion or fright, I didn't wait to see. Mrs. Pryor, as though she could restore tradition with volume, played louder.

Reverend Hough looked mildly surprised as I reached out to take Josh's hand and led him around the altar and up the side steps onto the chancel so that everyone could see us. My heart was pumping with the pulse I recognized as the genuine me, the one that had gotten flattened since I'd arrived back in Chisholm. There we were, me and my groom facing all the people in my parents' community. I looked down at the row of bride's maids on my right. My cousin Marianne, Deanna, and Calinda stood wide-eyed. The candle lighters had let their lighters droop to their sides. Olivia's beautiful face looked up at me. She was crying softly for herself or me or for the loss of a wedding she had put her faith in. Cassandra Zotikos, my Sandy, gave me a thumbs up.

"Not here. Not now," I whispered to Josh. "Trust me."

"Okay," he shrugged. "I knew something was up."

Mrs. Pryor was still pounding away. I raised my hand, but before I could catch her eye, Ernest had gotten to her, and with a dying swerve the music stopped.

I took a deep breath. Everyone was waiting to see what I would say, especially me. "You all are so beautifully dressed up—" I called out across the sanctuary. I was breathing hard but my volume was amazing. "—so I'm reluctant to tell you that there isn't going to be a wedding today. I'm so sorry." The crowd was stunned and silent, but I was suddenly feeling buoyant. "No," I shouted. "I *am* sorry to disappoint you, but I'm *not* sorry to call off this ceremony."

And with that I, who never cries, began to weep big sloppy tears in front of my third grade teacher and the mayor of Chisholm and my stunned mother and everyone who had come to see me tie the knot. "It's not that I've changed my mind about the groom," I sobbed loudly. "I love Josh and he and I are going to be together no matter what." A low murmur arose from the sanctuary. My view of the wedding guests dissolved as tears poured down my cheeks and dripped off my chin. I swung Josh's hand and smiled at him. I felt we might lift off and fly out one of the high open windows. "It's just that today is not the day!"

I smiled at the watery congregation. "There's lots of food and drink downstairs." I sang out. "And I know you'll have a lot to talk about."

THE END

Made in the USA
Charleston, SC
24 January 2013